Neither Liberty Nor Justice

The Last Days of Woodson and Calvin Blasingame

Harley Gamble

A biased and fictional account, albeit as true as some or most, of the 1856 killings of Woodson and Calvin Blasingame

-Harley Gamble

Dedication

To my inspiration, my detail driven wife Annette, and my favorite Texan, her brilliant and equally detail driven sister Ruthie.

ONE

German Cemetery, Blanco County, Texas
Yesterday afternoon, 2 PM

Arthritis kept the grandmother from opening the rusted gate with her left hand, so she pushed it with her elbow. It squeaked as it opened. After stepping through and examining her elbow for dirt or rust, she waved two grandchildren into the aged and abandoned cemetery's rising field. She and the children, a boy and a girl, held hands as they climbed through wilted bluebonnets, lines of worn gravestones, and dormant brown grass amid thriving tough weeds. Atop the hill, above the markers and weed knots, a lone live oak served as a solitary and windswept sentinel for buried Texicans and the eternity they faced. It sheltered a beckoning white iron bench.

The grandmother answered to 'Gree', so named by her oldest grandchild at age one. She led the children to the bench through a developing breeze and swept dust and loose white paint flecks away with her kerchief before she sat. "Find your kinfolk for me," she said.

Logan and Jojo, now ten and twelve, looped in separate circles;

he went north of Gree, and she circled south until Logan called, "None of these names sound American."

Gree knew why. "Most people buried here were German by birth and Texican by choice."

The explanation seemed to satisfy Logan. It opened more questions, too. He joined Gree at the bench and began quizzing her before he sat and peppered one quick question after another.

"Take a breath!" said Gree as she held up a hand. "We'll cover all of that. You know, someday you'll be a lawyer, a good one!"

"Aha!" Jojo called, interrupting them from twenty yards away. With considerable artistic flair, and she had plenty to spare, she planted her left foot and raised her left hand high. "I found them!" she shouted while curtseying. Jojo stood erect, laughed the victor's laugh, and flicked dark hair from her face before putting her hands on her hips. "Gree needed help from a strong and smart woman! That was me!" She made a spear-throwing motion that ended with an index finger pointed at her brother's heart. The gesture was vivid. Gree knew Jojo did it to add strength to her words.

Logan sneered. "Pa was talking about you when he said, 'Even a blind pig can find an acorn once in a while'." A dour expression painted his face as he walked toward the gravestone by his sister. After laying a hand on the marker, he dropped to his knees and tore weeds away from the overgrown bases, and the names they hid, as Gree neared. He touched the now exposed etchings. They were clean, undamaged by years of exposure. "Gree, somebody cut these American names deeper than the ones on most markers."

Gree knew why. "Makes you think somebody wanted them remembered, doesn't it?"

Logan said, "And they both died in the same year! Woodson

and Calvin are the father and son you meant that died together! You said there was a lot about them to know when we planned this trip."

Jojo continued her brother's thought. "And you promised you'd tell us why, what happened, when we got here."

Gree sorted details from her grandfather's account of the Blasingames before continuing. "Our being here together makes this a solemn moment; one not only for me, one for the three of us."

Jojo and Logan's bickering ended. They fell quiet.

Gree's voice became very soft as she said, "Listen as I read their names. Remember that we share their blood. We and these departed Blasingames are family, one and all. They are our kin." The children stood and closed their eyes as she said a brief prayer. After the prayer, Gree read the markers and said, "Woodson Blasingame, 1798-1856. Calvin Blasingame, 1831-1856."

Logan didn't raise his head as he peeked at his grandmother. "Tell us again how many greats are between Woodson and us."

Jojo pressed, "And I really want to hear everything that happened! I want to know everything they did, everything that happened to them, and why!"

Logan asked, "What did they do that made somebody want to kill them?"

Gree answered, "Logan, you asked two questions. As to how many greats, Woodson was my great, great, great Grandpa. Add two more greats for your and JoJo's relationship to him. To answer your second question, a mob killed them both. Murdered them describes what happened better."

"But why? Why would a mob, anybody, do something like that?" Jojo asked.

"It was an act of retribution fueled by misplaced rage."

"I know what retribution means," said Logan. "It means getting even with somebody."

Jojo pressed, "Why was the mob getting even with the Blasingames, Gree? You said you'd tell us more!"

Gree glanced at the sun. They still had over an hour of daylight. "I did say that. Are you ready to hear the story now?"

Jojo and Logan again answered as one. "We are!"

Gree organized her thoughts. Despite her 'every bit of everything' promise during their trip-planning session, she sanitized part of what she knew. She then told her grandchildren much of what happened over a hundred and seventy years ago.

Her account was gritty and more truthful than not, but she didn't share everything.

TWO

Blasingame home, Blanco County, Texas
Saturday, March 29, 1856, 5 PM

Woodson Blasingame sat on the circular stone wall surrounding the family well. He patted the space beside him as an invitation. Mary, his wife, sat beside her husband and touched his knee. It was an old signal that she had something to say. "Woodson, over the last thirty years, we've lived in South Carolina, Alabama, and Texas." She sighed. "I liked the first two, but I love Texas." She sighed and tightened her grip on his knee. Woodson knew she had more to say. "Two years ago, we chose this land well. It is fertile. We have hills to the east and west, agreeable German immigrants to our north, and dependable Scot Irish to our South. They are important in my life, but what's most important is Blanco County is where you are. It's where you built my castle and where we owe no money to nobody. Woodson, promise me something."

"Anything…"

"Promise we'll never move again."

"That's easy." The comforting sound of his soft laugh followed before he added, "That is an easy promise, Mary. I love the home you designed, and we built. I love you and this house enough to tell you when I leave it, I will go feet first."

***

As the sun touched the hill to their west, Mary stood and ran her fingers over the well's stone wall. She then brushed the back of her dress with both hands. "Those stones are hard!"

Woodson reached around her and clasped a butt cheek with each of his hands. "But you are soft..."

"I hope you'll do that again, after the children are asleep!" Mary laughed. "As for between now and then, I'm getting a bit chilly. Let's go inside."

The house was the product of Mary's thirty-year dream. It began with a few private rough sketches in South Carolina. She redrew, refined, and discussed her dream with Woodson, several times in Alabama, and he always assured her the day would come when they would have it. The dream neared reality not long after the Blasingames bought land in Texas in 1854, when Mary and Woodson sat together under the shade of a trio of live oaks. "This is what I want," she said while taking her drawing pad from her tow sack and opening it across her husband's lap. "I want a corner fireplace, an open area for family life, cooking and eating, and four bedrooms along the back wall." She pointed to the smaller sides of her drawn rectangle. "We need two shuttered windows on each shared area outer wall and one in each bedroom. By opening and closing shutters and doors, we can control light and ventilation during hot weather. In winter, we'll open or close some or all to regulate how much heat we get from the corner fireplace"

Woodson's only additions were a series of vertical slits he would cut and plug on both sides of every window. Should Lipan Apache raiders return to the area, the family could pull the plugs and defend themselves by shooting marauders through the openings. They'd be safe and unseen.

***

In the dining area, the Blasingame's oldest son Calvin arm-wrestled his brother Luther with little success at the dining table. Calvin was strong, he had been for years, but now Luther, although five years younger, was stronger.

After Luther pressed the back of his brother's hand to the table, Calvin leaned back in his chair, and stared at his mother. Neither she, now in the kitchen area, nor Calvin's teenage sister Sarah, offered sympathy. None from their younger brother Columbus, either. Instead, he slapped the checkerboard on the dining table's other end when the youngest brother, William, double-jumped him for yet another victory.

Motion outside, movement by someone or something well beyond the living area windows, pulled Columbus from his anguish. He recognized a lone figure on a familiar wagon at the far gate. It was Thomas Johnson standing on the mercantile wagon's bench seat moving his arms, waving toward the house. "Daddy, we got company out by the gate," said Columbus.

Calvin flexed his right bicep. It hurt as he came to Columbus' side. "Damn Luther is as strong as an ox," he said while looking out the window. He snorted; it was a derisive sound. He stepped out to the porch and gestured for Thomas to continue. He returned to the house, still flexing his right arm, and shook his head from side to side. "It's Thomas Johnson wavin' like a fool out at the gate! It ain't like we'd shoot him, even if he deserved it."

"How come we're always last delivered?" asked Columbus.

Calvin's grin showed his mischievous nature. "On account of that gives Thomas more time to moon over Sarah. You'll learn more about stuff like that when you get older."

"Is Thomas gonna take Sarah to the moon?'

"He'd like to do just that!"

Woodson ended his oldest son's performance. "That's enough, Calvin."

Columbus' question, Calvin's fresh answer, and her father's admonition combined to paint a blush on sixteen-year-old Sarah's face. A sharp clap of Mary's hands made certain that the conversation would not continue.

***

As Thomas neared the house, kitchen aromas, cooking chickens, sweet potatoes, and green beans followed Woodson and Calvin to the porch. Woodson raised his right hand and said, "Howdy, Thomas. How's your family doing?"

"They're all fine, Mister Blasingame, doing well." Thomas raised his nose in an exaggerated motion and blurted, "Something fine going on in the kitchen!" He pulled the mercantile wagon near the house and stopped by the porch steps.

"Boy's looking for a dinner invite," Calvin whispered to his father.

"I think I'll offer him one. I think Sarah may like that, too."

"Mister Blasingame, "said Thomas. "I got the whole of the order you gave Daddy the other day. We had everything you wanted in stock; we didn't have to order out for any of it." He jumped down, lowered his wagon's rear gate, and counted his wares for Woodson, just like his Daddy said for him to do. The Mercantile's oldest and most hard-fast rule was that every family's tally had to be right.

Woodson, his sun-darkened skin looked like leather after ten years under Alabama and Texas suns, stepped off the porch and walked to Thomas' side. The family's oldest son, the youthful and charming Calvin, did the same. Luther, the Blasingame's now stronger and more muscular second son, walked onto the porch to watch his father and older brother.

At the wagon, Calvin and Thomas made small talk as Woodson examined his merchandise and his bill. After a quick nod, Woodson declared it right and thanked Thomas for the licorice whips. "Our little ones love those things!"

Thomas didn't address the licorice. "Mr. Blasingame," he said, "Daddy asks that you square up with him the next time you're in town." He lowered his voice to explain. "It's a little embarrassing for me, but Daddy don't want me handling money."

Woodson exchanged quick stares with Calvin and Luther. Their father's unspoken message was 'Do not make jokes at Thomas' expense.' The brothers remained quiet and stone-faced as they took part of the stores inside and the rest to the root cellar.

Mary walked through the doorway and stopped beside Luther. Her striking appearance, that trim figure, those piercing blue eyes, and her mother's Cherokee cheekbones still penetrated her husband's heart every day. She pulled her now gray-streaked black hair into a bun. "Did we get everything we ordered?"

Thomas removed his hat. "Afternoon, Mrs. Blasingame! Yes, Ma'am, you did. I just told Mister Blasingame we had everything you wanted in stock!" He rubbed his nose. "Ain't a kitchen in Blanco County that smells as good as yours!"

"What a wonderful thing to say! Thank you, Thomas."

Thomas' eyes darted to Sarah as she joined her mother. More woman than child at sixteen, it was obvious to Woodson, and anyone else who looked, that Sarah's beautiful face, violet eyes, and raven hair beguiled Thomas.

Sarah clasped her hands together. "Good evening, Thomas. It's good to see you again."

Woodson watched his daughter's lips move within the smile she aimed at Thomas. *Did she just say, 'so handsome'? Thomas? Handsome?*

"Good evening, Miss Sarah. It's good to see you again, too." Color rose on Thomas' neck and covered his face. His lips continued to move, but no other words passed over his lips.

The boy's dumbstruck, thought Woodson.

Thomas' flushed face, neck, and arms took control of his mind and tongue. "I wasn't sure. I mean, I think that's the first time you ever called me by my name." He folded his arms across his chest. "Well, you may have. I don't recall. I mean I guess I don't know…"

Sarah pulled Thomas from his maelstrom. "We have plenty of everything for supper tonight, Thomas. If Momma and Daddy approve, you're welcome to stay for dinner." She paused, smiled again, and looked at her father. "Daddy?" she asked.

"You're more than welcome, Thomas," said Woodson.

"If you'd like and have time," added Sarah. She smiled again.

Thomas said, "Oh, yes sir, Mister Blasingame. Thank you, Miss Sarah! I have plenty of time and thank you for the invite, sir!"

Calvin and Luther covered smirks with their hands and did so without obvious ridicule. They knew their father didn't have to look straight at them to be watching and listening. Woodson sympathized with the depth of Thomas' mute and lovesick purgatory. He was young enough at heart to remember the joy, concern, and apprehensions that tormented young males.

Out of earshot of everyone, Calvin's Puck broke free of his father's unspoken threat. He leaned near Thomas' ear. "Don't let Pa or me catch you looking at Sarah's backside if she stoops to take something out of the oven! Something like that would haunt you the rest of your life, which wouldn't be long if daddy sees it, or if I do and tell daddy what you done."

Thomas nodded. He did not speak.

***

Mary clapped her hands twice for attention. She instructed Columbus, "Tend to Thomas' team. When you finish, wash your hands with soap and water and fetch your bedroom chair to the table. Thomas will have your regular seat tonight."

Columbus walked to the wagon. There he turned toward the porch, ignored his father shaking his head from side to side, and contorted his face into a smarter-than-you grin. "Momma, I know why I'm the one what's gotta get a chair for dinner. It's because Sarah wants to sit beside Thomas, ain't it?" He smirked. Columbus' words splashed new color on Thomas' face and neck.

Mary invited Thomas to go inside and wash his hands in the kitchen. When she heard water splash in the sink, she clapped her hands for Columbus' further attention. She got it.

With pursed lips, a pointing finger under an icy smile, and a single raised eyebrow. she froze Columbus. It was a series of gestures Columbus, indeed all the Blasingame children, knew and understood. The boy's mother had charged, tried, and convicted him on all charges. Columbus had to know that his life would take a sad turn when Thomas left.

"I need to learn to shut up," Columbus sighed. He continued to the barn.

Mary wiped her hands on her apron and went inside.

***

Sarah returned to the porch as her mother entered the house. Her eyes caught Columbus' as he closed the barn door. He showed concern as he walked slow, measured steps while nearing his sister. Sarah softened him with a smile that looked real when he touched the hitching rail. He continued with more confident steps. When they were side by side, Sarah locked her right hand on his left elbow and dropped to one knee. He resisted to no avail as she pulled him close and whispered to him. In a soft voice, one only Columbus could hear, she said, "I should have strangled you when I had a chance. I won't make that mistake again!"

At dinner, Thomas sat between Sarah and her mother. When Sarah's knee touched his for a fleeting, almost nonexistent moment, he blinked.

I ain't lucky enough for her to do that on purpose.

Two seats away, on Mary's right, Nancy waved her licorice whip. "Thank you for this, Thomas." She laid it by her plate.

Thomas brushed Sarah's knee while leaning forward. "You're welcome, Nancy. I'm glad you like it," he answered. *Hope that touch wasn't too much!*

Nancy rubbed her stomach with both hands when it growled. After a giggle, she tugged at her mother's sleeve. "When is Daddy going to talk to his plate? My stomach just said I want to eat."

Mary looked at Woodson. "My dear...?" she asked.

Woodson bowed his head. "Lord, like the children of Israel, you led us to a Promised Land. Ours is Texas. Like them, we come with hope, love of You, and faith in your Ten Commandments. Tonight, as we eat from your bounty, we pledge our faith anew and ask you to watch over Thomas as he goes home. Amen."

Eight Amens followed. Ten seconds later, bowls and dishes

clinked as food circled the table. A few quick statements and questions of little import opened the gates of a sea of conversation. Observations, remarks, and asides floated up, down, and across the table. All were light, some were clever, and most were family and community oriented. Everyone except Thomas took part. Although his lips moved now and again, he remained silent.

Mary tugged on Woodson's sleeve and then whispered in his ear. "We need to make sure Thomas feels welcome. I'm going to draw him into the conversation." Woodson's agreeing nod was all but imperceptible.

"Thomas," she asked with a smile, "tell us of your Momma and Daddy. We hope all is well with them. How are they and what's going on in town?"

Thomas' neck reddened again. His eyes grew big before he squinted and answered in a hurried voice, "They're all fine, Mrs. Blasingame. They are doin' good; yes, ma'am." Thomas' lips barely moved as he counted "94-93-92-91..."

Mary nodded and fell silent. A moment later, she leaned close to Woodson's ear. "I think Thomas is counting backward from a hundred."

Woodson read Thomas' lip movements. "87-86-85... He whispered, "The boy may not be a good choice for Sarah after all."

Neither Blasingame knew why Thomas heard little of or ignored the casual talk around the table, because the culprit was under the table. It was Sarah's knee. When she had touched it to Thomas', he entered a state of hormone-driven frenzy.

Thomas clenched his teeth. "66-65-64-63..."

Calvin wiped his mouth and slapped his belly. "Daddy, Momma," he said before a sigh, "I got something to say that I shouldn't in front of company." Quiet encircled the table as the oldest Blasingame son looked at his father. "Callahan fired me yesterday afternoon. He fired me for being a no-account, which I ain't!"

"What did 'no-account' mean when he was firing you?" asked Woodson.

Thomas' eyes darting from son to father and back told Woodson he didn't want to hear any of this.

Calvin continued, "It wasn't even about me. The old coot called us no-accounts because you and Luther talked bad to the Germans about him gettin' after the Mexicans and Indians. He said no white man should criticize his own to no German for no reason, including killin' raiders and savages!"

Luther answered, "I only talk about James Callahan around home! I ain't said nothin' to nobody else nowhere about him!"

Calvin laughed aloud, "You should have seen the blood vessels pop out on his head and neck while he screamed about trying to be nice! He'd done fired me by then, so it was all I could do to keep from laughing when he said the Lipans wouldn't listen."

Mary clapped her hands once. "You will show respect for your elders in this house! No matter what you feel about him, James Callahan is our age, not yours!"

Luther spoke up. "What you said about us and the Ten Commandments, it don't mean nothin' to Mister Callahan. If it did, he'd have remembered that number six in Exodus says don't murder! He killed women and old men from ambush and never batted an eye! His words and deeds don't fit together. They have not true written all over them!"

Woodson said, "Let Calvin speak right now, Luther. Give him a chance to finish what he wants to say."

Luther shook his head and looked into his father's eyes. "Daddy, I was there, and I saw what he done. It's why I'll never ride with him again!"

"That's enough, Luther."

***

Thomas was old enough to understand irony when it slapped him hard enough. Sarah again touched her knee to his as her Daddy said, "We avoid sin and sinful thoughts in this house."

Although Sarah wasn't anybody's wife, it was obvious to Woodson that Thomas coveted her.

***

Nancy waved her licorice whip and smiled as her father continued. "And we have no liars in this house, either! Have I talked with the Germans about James? I have! Did I gossip? I did not. You know Callahan blusters, runs hot and cold, but that's just him." Woodson softened his voice. "He'll be out here Monday wanting to hire you back!"

That was when Calvin proved he either could not recognize victory or avoided it to continue conflict. "Well, I got to say that ain't the only burr under that old Ranger's saddle. He said he didn't like the way me and Mrs. Callahan look at one another and he wonders about it."

Sarah spooned a plump piece of white meat and two carrots into Thomas' bowl.

He ate it with his eyes closed.

"She's too good looking for him, anyway. Lots of people around here think that but nobody will say it," continued Calvin.

Color returned to Thomas' neck as Woodson pressed Calvin. "Are you doin' anything with Mrs. Callahan? Company or no company, tell me now!"

Luther spoke up before Calvin could answer. "I know you told me I'd said enough, daddy, but if one of them lurked on the other, it was her,"

"… And nothing happened between me and her! I ain't never even shook hands with Mrs. Callahan," said Calvin

Woodson's voice sounded more relaxed as he answered. "Then she'll convince James he's wrong about you and he'll get mad at somebody else."

Calvin raised a finger as though he had more to say. Mary stopped him with a quick, "Your father said he'd want to hire you back; end of story."

Woodson took charge of the conversation. "Until then, the best way for us to avoid trouble is for you boys, and by boys I mean Calvin and Luther, to be where it ain't. I want both of you to work at home until this all settles out. Stay away from the saloon, too. Don't go for even one beer!" He took a deep breath. "While you're working, plan a hunting trip! We need meat."

Mary added, "And we don't need trouble."

"I reckon I said more than I should, talkin' misery over dinner and all," said Calvin.

Ain't that the truth rolled through Woodson's mind.

That relief proved short-lived when Calvin stunned every adult for a second time. "I always asked if any of James' kids were Grudge Babies," he asked aloud. "I never said that to anybody else. I reckon I'm glad I didn't!"

"What's a Grudge Baby?" asked Mary.

Woodson knew the old joke. He leaned near Mary's ear, but his whisper was louder than he thought. "Somebody had it in for him!"

Thomas closed his eyes and folded his hands in his lap.

The females, save the oblivious Nancy, sat with their spoons frozen in midair.

Columbus made things worse. "Had what in?" he asked.

Mary said, "Close your mouth when you chew, Columbus," The eyebrow and icy smile turned toward Calvin. "I will tolerate no vulgarity in this house!"

Racing apologies ensued. Woodson thought most of them made sense under the circumstances, although some, meaning both of Calvin's, sounded crazy. Everyone seemed to relax after Calvin's final effort. It ended the conversation for good.

***

Thomas alone enjoyed a redeeming grace. The tent Sarah's knee put in his pants disappeared.

THREE

Callahan Ranch, Blanco County, Texas
Tuesday, April 1, 1856, 1 PM

Judgmental and grizzled behind the forfeited Ranger's Star he still wore, James Callahan weighed right and wrong on an unforgiving scale. He was a proud man, a confident one, whose vainglorious streak prompted him to remind others often of his wisdom and exploits. On more than one occasion, he told his wife with a straight face that he often felt like a nineteenth--century Solomon.

Sarah, James' wife, questioned his claim in her diary. One entry read *Thank God the real Solomon didn't have your temper.*

Twenty years before, James earned Blanco County's settlers' admiration when his homegrown militia bested a battalion of troublesome Mexican soldiers. The settlers' affection grew five years later when he crossed the Rio Grande leading revenge raiding parties against the Lipan Apaches. His militia matched the Lipans raid for raid until the Apaches lost interest in Blanco County.

James's outdoor adventures and general rough living gave

him a harsh leather-skinned appearance, one that matched his demeanor. Those traits offered stark contrasts to his wife's, and fodder for the untraceable rumors that she, a widow with two small children, married him for money. He hated those stories, worried about them, and was quick to respond to insults and challenges to his marriage, even when they didn't exist.

FOUR

Callahan Ranch, Blanco County, Texas
Thursday, April 3, 1856, 10 AM

James Callahan pushed his coffee cup across the kitchen table. "I hear wagons; sounds like two of them,"

Eli Hines, James' most devoted friend, set his cup beside James' and said, "Thank you, Sarah," as she took them to the sink.

"You're welcome, Eli. James, I have a week's worth of sewing to do. Call me if you need me." She left the room.

James walked to the door and watched 'Mallheel' Johnson, in the lead wagon, look over his right shoulder and raise his left hand, It was a signal to his son, Thomas, to stop the mercantile's second wagon, As Thomas did so, Mallheel cupped his left hand by his mouth, stared at the kitchen door and shouted, "James Callahan! It's Mallheel! Me and my boy have your supplies!"

James shook his head. "Eli, that stupid son-of-a bitch is shouting at me while we stare at one another twenty feet apart" He passed a quick grin to his still seated friend before adding, "But he's on time every time. I have to say that for him."

Sarah returned from her sewing room and glanced at Mallheel through the kitchen window. "His son is with him today; Thomas seems like a nice boy," she said.

"Thomas does seem like a good boy," answered James. He gestured to his friend. "Come with me, Eli," As Eli stood, James stepped onto the kitchen stoop and walked across the sunbaked dirt to the wagons. He pulled each wagon's tarp away and took a cursory look into each bed. and said, "It looks right. Thomas, you know where to put everything." As Thomas carried some boxes and bags to the cellar and others to the kitchen, James pulled a sheet of paper from his shirt pocket. "Mallheel, my note says you quoted me forty dollars even..."

"And forty it is, my friend!" agreed Mallheel.

Callahan gave Mallheel two twenty-dollar gold pieces. Johnson wrote 'paid gold in full' and then signed James' receipt.

James returned the 'paid' note to his pocket. He then turned to Sarah, who remained at the kitchen window. "Will you put a fresh pot of coffee on for us? Eli and I want to visit with these fellows for a bit."

Sarah made coffee as Eli, Mallheel, and Thomas sat at the kitchen's round dining table. When the coffee was ready, James said, "Before you leave us, hand me the unopened whiskey jug from under the sink."

She brought it to James. He set the jug in the table's center and watched Sarah fill cups with coffee. After Sarah served them, she smiled first at her husband and then at his guests before returning to her sewing room.

Around the kitchen table, talk began with the weather. It followed a familiar pattern when it shifted to memories of fighting the Mexicans and Indians before settling on Texas independence.

"You know, we'd be part of Mexico or Indian country if we hadn't done what we done," said James. "We made Texas, not them damned politicians!"

Mallheel voiced a loud accolade. "That's right! That's a fact! You a hero! Eli, too!" He filled his cup with whiskey before he added, "You ought to be a hero to the Blasingames, too! You know, Thomas delivered an order out there last Saturday. He ate supper with them, too."

James picked up the jug and topped the other three cups. After returning the whiskey to the table's center, he snorted, "Sumbitch Blasingame talks shit about me with his German friends. He don't appreciate me saving his family's ass by killing Indian and Mexican raiders that were out to kill them! Humility! A man needs it, and Woodson Blasingame has none! Good men have cut many a braying ass to size for that kind of smart-ass behavior. Woodson, his boy Calvin, too, need to appreciate more and talk less. If Woodson don't, the day will come when his half-breed wife and adopted young'uns will need another daddy."

Thomas stammered, "Mrs. Blasingame, she is a good cook! I think better'n Momma..."

"Don't go blaspheming your momma's cookin', boy! Don't compare her unfavorable to no mixed-blood squaw in no way!" said Mallheel. He added more whiskey to his cup. After snorting once, he glared at his son. "Thomas, tell Mister Callahan what you heard over dinner that evening."

Thomas shook his head. "There ain't nothin' much to tell. They talked about the usual stuff like family, farming, and the like."

Mallheel tightened his eyes and pressed his finger on the table in front of his son. "You know what I expect from you! Tell it."

"Who said what, Thomas?" asked Callahan. "You'll not get in

trouble telling the truth."

Thomas said, "Calvin said you fired him for nothing; that you accused him of messing with Mrs. Callahan and he did no such thing. Luther agreed with him."

James measured his words. "One fact is I fired the bastard. Another is that I wouldn't believe Calvin if he said it's raining in a thunderstorm. He's a liar and his claim about him not tryin' to get on my wife proves it." He finished his cup, and added, "I got no proof of that, but I know the truth! The truth talks to me! As for Luther, I don't blame him. He spoke up for his brother and even stupid people got no choice when it comes to defending blood. As for Woodson and Calvin, Woodson's big mouth makes him untrustworthy, but Calvin's worse. That young buck chases other men's women. I know that in my heart!"

Thomas asked, "Daddy, shouldn't we head to the store? We got work waiting for us."

Mallheel glared at Thomas. "When I say so, boy! Now, tell Mister James the joke they made about his children, his real ones, not the ones he adopted."

Thomas paled, groped for words. "Wadd'n nothing much; it was just some after-dinner funnin'. Ain't worth the air to talk about it."

James fumed, tapped his knuckles on the table "Young fellow, talk now!"

Thomas' voice quivered. "I told daddy a stupid joke Calvin told at dinner." He stared at his father. "I won't do that again!" He looked at James, shrugged his shoulders, and continued, "It embarrassed Mrs. Blasingame and their daughter Sarah. Mrs. Blasingame dressed Calvin down for it. There was nothing to it. Ain't a secret in this county that sometimes Calvin talks silliness. That was one of those times."

"This is your last warning, boy," hissed Mallheel.

Thomas nodded. "All right," he said before continuing, "Calvin said since Mister Callahan was gone so much, he meant fighting Indians and all..." He fell silent.

"Damn, Thomas, help me here," said James.

Thomas swallowed. He then blurted, "Calvin said he suspected that Mr. Callahan's children were 'Grudge Babies'."

James' brow furrowed. "I never heard of such a thing. What the hell is a Grudge Baby?"

Thomas whispered, "The joke means that 'somebody had it in for you'."

James needed no more explanation. He threw his coffee cup into the kitchen fireplace. As the whiskey burned blue, he walked to the wall hooks by the fireplace and removed his gun belt.

Eli Hines, the only man in Blanco County James considered his equal, walked to his friend and lay a hand on James' shoulder.

James stood still and listened. He would have done that for no one else, not even his Sarah.

Eli said, "Put that back and let me talk to Blasingame. No offense to either Johnson, but Thomas' story don't sound right to me. Let me see Woodson myself, hear what he has to say, before you do anything. I'll tell you everything I learn. You already know I'll tell you the truth. We can discuss everything after that."

James grunted but didn't speak. His eyes darted back and forth.

Eli continued, "What I'm about to say is important, James. I hope you'll listen because you're mad right now and we both know you don't make your best decisions when you go off like that."

James clinched and unclenched his fists. "Go on," he said.

"Whatever you think the Blasingames said or did may or may not be true. One thing that is true, is that they aren't marauders or troublemakers, none of them. Most of Blanco County, damn near everybody, will tell you they're an upstanding family, one folk around here like a lot! If you go after an innocent Blasingame without good reason, and right now you don't have one, your reputation, your life around here, will suffer. Your wife will feel it worse than you if you act out of hand, too. Some of the church women, and you know who I mean, would shun her."

James' voice took on a cold, hard edge. "Grudge baby, Eli? Are you telling me you'd take a slap at your wife like that?"

Eli continued in a soft voice. "I'd do what I want you to do. Let a good friend find out what happened before I did anything else."

James looked around the room.

"If me talkin' to Woodson can lay the groundwork for resolving this, that's the path to follow," said Eli. "Should our talkin' lead to nothing, so be it. I'll tell anybody that asks that you made sure what you heard was true before you did anything."

"All right, all right!" James said. He waved a finger sideways in front of his nose and blurted, "I ain't happy, but do it! If what Thomas said proves true, I'll do no forgivin' and may not accept an apology! I'll want Woodson and Calvin's asses gone! If either of them defies or smartasses me, I'll kill 'em both! Understood?"

"I understand, and I'll address everything that concerns you." Eli reached across the table and touched Mallheel's arm. "This ain't personal, but you and Thomas need to go. James and I need a private moment, Mallheel."

Mallheel pledged help and loyalty to Callahan.

"And keep quiet about what you heard here," said Eli.

"Wouldn't think about doing nothing else," answered Mallheel.

***

When the wagons were out of earshot, Thomas pulled his team beside his father's. "What I told you was a private remark, son to father. I can't believe you told Mister Callahan what I said!"

Mallheel's grip on his reins tightened.

Thomas added, "And I'll stop you from making it worse if I can, Daddy. I ain't makin' trouble for no Blasingame because I aim to marry their Sarah someday. If I angered up her family, she'd shed me on the spot. She wouldn't have no choice!"

Mallheel pursed his lips and pointed a finger at his son. "You have grown a big mouth, Thomas! If you defy me, I'll beat the Hell out of you, boy! That last beatin' won't be nothin' beside what I'll do to you next time!" After a brief but weighted quiet, Mallheel asked, "Anything else you want to say?"

Thomas didn't answer. He stared straight ahead and urged his team forward. Neither he nor his father spoke as they passed through James Callahan's gate.

***

At the kitchen door, James and Eli watched the Johnsons turn onto the farm-to-market road. They returned to the kitchen table, where Eli rested his elbows and took a deep breath. "I need to say something you already know about Mallheel, James."

"I always want your opinion, Eli. You know that."

"If you ever doubted that Mallheel Johnson is the stupidest son-of-a-bitch in Blanco County, he proved it this morning! He had no reason to stir up shit about something he can't prove, and his boy said was nothing! Instead, he started strutting and preening, running his mouth, without knowing his facts! All he did today was show his ass! You and I both know that!"

"Mallheel bein' a dumbass ain't my problem! Even a dumbass

tells the truth once in a while. If this was Mallheel's once in a while, Woodson and Calvin have made themselves my problem."

"You make good sense when you're calm, and I thought you were headed that way. I can see that you aren't there yet," said Eli. "Maybe this will help." He poured more whiskey in his and James' cups. He then slammed his fist on the table as hard as he could. Both cups jumped, but neither spilled a drop. "I 'm pissin' up a rope tryin' to reason with you when you don't control yourself, and you are yet to take that step!" They locked eyes. This time James looked away first. Eli said, "Mallheel pressured hell out of Thomas. That alone raises doubt."

"It does." James' voice had calmed.

"If Thomas' story is true, if Calvin was insulting, I'll tell you. If I think ain't nothin' to it, I'll tell you that, too. What you'll get from me is what you always get. The truth."

"That's all I can ask," said James. "And if Mallheel's right, I need to know if you're with me."

"If it's more than Mallheel stirring shit or youngsters being stupid, I'll help you make things right." Eli finished his drink, walked to the sink, and set his China cup on the counter. After glancing at the closed sewing room door, he looked to James. Neither spoke. Eli said, "Tell Sarah I appreciate the coffee."

James nodded.

Eli walked outside, mounted his horse, and started toward home.

FIVE

Blasingame home, Blanco County, Texas
Saturday, April 5, 1856, 4 PM

Someone or something at the far gate caught Woodson's eye as he cleaned and sharpened Mary's knives on the porch. He shaded his eyes with his left hand and a hard squint helped identify their visitor. He carried the knives and his daddy's sharpening stone inside through the front door and laid them beside the sink. "Eli Hinds is coming. He just passed through the gate!"

He looked through the kitchen window. Still a distance away, Eli Hinds approached the house. "Mary," asked Woodson, "Will you put on a pot of coffee?" He turned to Columbus. "Wait for him on the front stoop, son. Invite Mister Hinds inside and tell him we made fresh coffee."

The boy returned to the porch. As Eli drew near, Columbus waved and called, "Daddy says come in, Mister Hinds. Momma just made some fresh coffee."

Eli didn't dismount. "Tell your daddy I appreciate it but I'm short on time today. Ask if I can join him for coffee next time and I'd appreciate it if he'd join me out here today, just the two of us.

Tell him I won't take much of his time."

Woodson joined Columbus on the porch. "Are you sure you don't have time for coffee, Eli? Mary makes a good pot and this one is fresh brewed."

Columbus asked, "Can I listen while you and Mister Hines talk? I won't say anything. All I I want to do is listen."

"Not this time, son. Go into the house." Woodson tousled the boy's hair. Columbus went inside and watched his father and Eli Hines through the living area window.

Outside, a few quiet seconds grew into a half minute before Woodson asked, "What's on your mind, Eli? I doubt you came this far to turn down coffee and stare at my front door."

Eli shifted his weight in his saddle. "I want to set up a private talk, something on neutral ground, for you and James Callahan. He has hard feelings about spoken words, and nothing settles a dispute like honest talk between fair men."

Woodson stuck his thumbs in his belt loops. "I've done nothing to James Callahan and said nothing I wouldn't say to his face. What's he mad about?"

"…He has two complaints. One neither of you'll dispute is you talked bad about him with the Germans."

Woodson freed his thumbs and sat on his porch. "Being neighbors, I told them some things that concerned me. One was James' treatment of old Mexicans and Indians, including women. I shared that what he done disgusted me as much as it did them. I wasn't spreading secrets, Eli. Hell, you know as well as I do that James brags about it in the saloon every week!"

Eli untied his kerchief and mopped his brow. "That's true." He retied the kerchief before he spoke again. "Something else that's true is that he gets out of control every now and when he does, bad things can happen. That's what happened when he killed those old Mexicans and Indians." Eli took a deep breath. "I'm not asking you to excuse their deaths or anything else."

"What you are doing is beating around the bush, Eli."

"That's true," answered Eli. He scratched his nose before adding, "I don't want no craziness between you and James. Since you're the more reasonable of the two of you, I came to talk, to reason."

"I appreciate that. Say what you came to say, Eli."

"Weigh the good he's done for Blanco County against the bad on the fairest scales you can find. We both know it'll come out showing James does a lot more good than bad, a whole lot more."

"I ain't lookin' for trouble, Eli, but let me ask about what you're measuring. Answer this, what's lower than a man who kills old women?"

Hinds ignored the question. "He's done a lot of good for Blanco County. Good for the Blanco County Blasingames, too. Ask yourself how many times he saved us from Mexican and Indian raiders. He's done that more times than you can count."

"It sounds like you're trying to make James look reasonable before you get to the second of his irritations. When we lived in South Carolina, that meant it was the main one." Woodson. quit talking and waited.

"You could have been a lawyer," answered Eli after a shallow laugh. "James' wife is a beautiful woman, nobody'd deny that, and James gets jealous now and again. Jealous fears bring out the worst in him." Eli paused and then continued, "None of his fears about her and other men have ever been true, but that don't matter to him. To James, they ain't got to be true."

At last, thought Woodson. "Did James' wife give him a reason to question Calvin?"

"No. What happened was Mallheel and his boy delivered goods to Callahan while I was there last Thursday. We got to drinking and Mallheel got stupid from James' bourbon."

"Drunk...," said Woodson.

"Drunk enough to make Thomas tell everything you folks said over Saturday dinner. The part that made James craziest was the joke about him raising grudge babies."

"Calvin made that joke, and his momma ate him alive for it. I can tell you it won't be repeated around here. As for Thomas repeating anything that would reflect poor on our family, he's way too sweet on our Sarah to do that, even for his daddy."

Eli explained, "Mallheel pushed the boy hard, threatened him. The fool was drunk, saw a chance to promote himself to a customer, his biggest one, and took it." He then added, "James knows a fool when he sees one, and that's what Mallheel is, as you and I know, too. You and James can talk straight to one another, work this out with no third party involved. That means no me and no Mallheel. I ask you to meet with and talk to James. I ask as your friend and his."

"The whole thing irritates the Hell out of me, but I'll talk to keep the peace."

"Good... good!" answered Eli.

Woodson continued. "...But I won't go anywhere to do it. I won't look like I got my hat in my hand. Set it up for us to talk here. The false flag of truce he used on the Apaches is something I'll remember until the day I die and it's reason enough for me or anybody else to distrust him. When we talk, I'll show respect if James does. That includes me not carrying a gun if he don't, but if I see iron on his hip, I'll wear one, too. That'll be up to him."

Eli nodded. He turned his horse and left without another word.

<h1 style="text-align:center">SIX</h1>

Callahan Ranch, Blanco County, Texas
Monday, April 7, 1856, 9 AM

James Callahan's rage transformed to cold hate Monday morning. A row with his wife at the breakfast table ended with her sobbing in the sewing room and James ignoring her cries. He strapped a revolver to his hip and went out onto the kitchen porch. There he and his dog, a shaggy and sharp eared mutt, waited for James' friends.

When the dog stood and barked toward the distant gate, James knew that Eli Hinds and the Johnsons, Mallheel and Thomas, were nearby. When the threesome stopped their horses at the rail, James noticed that the Johnsons carried holstered pistols and their saddle sheaths held long rifles. Eli alone was unarmed. "You with me or not, Eli? Why aren't you armed?"

"We already been through this a couple of times, James. We're goin' over there to talk, not fight. Woodson's ready to resolve this peaceful and he gave me his word he'd be unarmed if you were."

"I've decided not to chance walking into a trap. If you're co-min', get a revolver off the hooks by the fireplace and a rifle from my cabinet. If you don't want to do that, you might as well head home."

"Alright," sighed Eli. He entered the house, strapped a holstered gun to his hip, and took a rifle and a box of cartridges from the cabinet's top drawer. As Eli returned and mounted his horse beside James and the Johnsons, a series of wails erupted from the house.

No one asked a question. James said, "Eli, I ain't mad at you and I talked rougher than I should have to an old friend. I apologize for that. Know that I intend to follow through on the talkin' commitment I made to you. "He then nodded toward the Blasingame spread, and grunted, "Let's go."

SEVEN

Blasingame home, Blanco County, Texas
Monday, April 7, 1856, 10:30 AM

Luther ran to the house. "Daddy, riders are heading toward the house. They just passed the gate."

From a chair by the still smoldering fireplace, Woodson asked, "You recognize them?"

Luther looked through the kitchen window. "It's James Callahan, Eli Hinds, and both Johnsons, Mallheel and Thomas. They're about halfway from the gate."

"Are they carrying guns?"

"I can't tell," answered Luther. "I know they didn't see me."

Calvin laid the splitting maul and honing stone by the back door and walked to the kitchen window. "They're wearing side-arms." He turned to face his father.

"Eli, too?"

"Eli and Mallheel are wearing gun belts. They have rifles hanging off their saddles, too."

"Didn't expect that from Eli..."

Sarah walked to Calvin's side. She touched Mary's arm when

she recognized Thomas. "Momma…"

Mary said, "Woodson, boys, let James blow off steam uninterrupted. After he hollers a while, he'll get over it, whatever it is, and go home." She walked to her husband. "All you have to do is let him scream! Nobody'll get hurt if you do! Nobody!"

Woodson went to the front window, where he watched the riders halt their mounts twenty yards from the house. He gestured for Mary to step away from the window before telling his sons. "I'm surprised to see Eli armed, but I doubt he had much choice after James got through with him." He walked to a point between the front door and living area window. "With them being armed out there, this isn't settin' up like a story with a happy ending, but that ain't got to be how it ends up. It's just what I see right now." He pointed a finger at Calvin and Luther, one after the other. "Me and James will do the talking today and you two won't. Your jobs are to keep quiet, watch me for directions, and don't get stupid. Any questions?" There were none. Woodson walked to the wall hooks by the leftmost bedroom and took down his and the oldest sons gun belts. He tossed Calvin's and Luther's to them before tying his holster to his thigh. "The only reason we're wearing these is that Callahan and his friends are wearing theirs. We'll not shoot if we have a choice and I'll make that decision. In plain talk, nobody shoots without me saying so or shooting first! Understand?" When no one spoke, he added, "Pull the wall plugs."

The boys answered, "Yes, Sir," in unison before separating and walking to the wall plugs on either side of the front window. They pulled them and waited.

Woodson kissed Mary's cheek. "You and Sarah take the young'uns to their bedroom and lock the door behind you. I don't want them out in the open if anything happens." His attention returned to the men beyond the front window, where James Callahan appeared uneasy on a nervous horse in front of Mallheel, Thomas, and Eli. James cupped his hands around his saddle horn and leaned forward. "Hello in the house!" he shouted.

Behind Woodson, Mary said, "Sarah, help me round up the little ones." The bedroom door made no sound as it closed behind them.

Woodson walked to the door, opened it enough for him to make eye contact with Callahan, and growled, "How come you wearin' a gun?"

"Because I don't trust you. You proved why when you pulled your window plugs."

"The reason I did is hanging on your hip. I told Eli I'd talk unarmed if you would, but that Colt says you aren't interested in that!" Woodson watched James' eyes trace the front and kitchen windows where the plugs had been during the hard following silence It ended when Woodson added, "Neither of us is deaf, so speak you piece. When you finish, I'll say mine. I hope we can find a solution."

James sounded calm. "I like to see a man's face when I'm negotiating with him. I learn as much that way as I do from what he says." An edge jumped into his voice. "Why don't you step out here and talk to me face to face? I heard you were gutless, and your boys were just like you."

Woodson answered with a hard edge of his own. "Drop the guns first. We need proof we ain't walkin' into one of your false flag traps, like the old Mexicans and Indians did. You slaughtered old women that day, didn't you James? I know you remember the butcherin' I'm talking about, It cost you your Ranger's Star."

Red faced Callahan sneered to Eli, "You call this workin' something out?"

Woodson pressed his point. "Git or talk and then git!"

James shouted, "By God, I come and go as I please in Blanco County, including right here." His angry hands trembled, and his neck held its bright red color. "You shouting from behind window plugs and women's skirts shows what you are, Blasingame! I ought to do the decent people of Blanco County a favor and evict your ass! You're a coward and Calvin's worse because he covets other men's wives!"

Eli rebuked both James and Woodson. "We came to talk, not rail like fools" an instant before a fly buzzed Callahan's nose and flitted to his thumb.

"Hush, Eli," snapped James while watching the fly dart to his revolver handle, back to his thumb, and again to the revolver's handle. He tried to swat it with a quick slap that landed on his revolver's grip.

Woodson, Calvin, and Luther never saw the fly. Woodson hissed, "Watch me; follow my lead. If we shoot, I shoot first!"

The fly tried to land on Mallheels horse's nose. The horse whinnied, tried to stand on its hind legs, and Malheel yanked the reins and sprayed loud curses toward the house. Calvin disregarded his father's warning and opened fire. Luther did the same seconds later. Three of their five rounds struck Callahan's head and chest. James slumped and fell with a thud as a frightened Mallheel Johnson levered three rifle shots toward the window slit to his right.

Woodson responded by firing through the now open door. Bone shards from Woodson's first shot shattered Mallheel's shoulder, dug into his horse's rump. Woodson's second shot burst Mallheel's skull and twisted the merchant's face into a grotesque smile while painting Thomas' face with blood.

"Back of daddy's head's gone!" screamed young Johnson as his father fell and rolled facedown near James. "Sweet Jesus, help me," screamed Thomas as he fired six shots into the wood beam over the front window before his horse spooked and bolted.

Woodson shouted to his sons, "Stop shooting! Leave Thomas and Eli alone! Neither of them shot at us!" His words came too late for Eli. Calvin had fired two shots as his father spoke. The first broke Eli's right arm and the second punctured his neck. His horse ran. Eli held the reins with his left hand and blood pulsed from his neck.

Two dead and two wounded and running presaged a grim silence as the Blasingames walked out to the porch. Woodson clinched his fist. He spoke first. "Damn it, both of you! What the Hell were you thinking?"

Calvin blurted in a nervous and fast voice. "I wanted to beat his ass but not this! God Almighty! What do we do, Daddy?"

"We'll leave them where they are, dead in front of our house with fired guns. That proves they came to fight after I agreed to meet unarmed. We did what Exodus teaches us to do when a sinner comes to take our eye. We took theirs first." Woodson walked to the bodies. "Calvin, Luther. For God's sake!"

Luther spoke in an uneasy voice. "He drew on us! You saw him, Daddy!"

Calvin agreed. "When James went for his gun, we shot his crazy ass! We didn't kill him on purpose. We shot after that hot head drew on us!"

Woodson recalled James' hand movement toward the revolver. It both looked like a draw and didn't at the same time. the hand movement had been quick, but it was unusual; more like a slap at the handle than trying to grip it. Still... James was a hot head who provoked and endangered Woodson's family with a gun at what was organized as a weapon free discussion. His boys had defended their momma, him, their younger brothers and sisters, and their home. That settled the matter for him.

Mary, Sarah, and the smaller children joined them, Mary and Sarah gasped as Woodson explained, "It was self-defense. James and his friends drew on us, tried to surprise us. When folks see them where they lay, they'll know we defended our own. James got what he came to do to us. The blame is on him. All of it."

Mary said she wanted to lie on the couch and returned to the house. Woodson followed her and sat in a nearby chair.

Luther, Calvin, and the small children stayed on the steps.

EIGHT

Blasingame home, Blanco County, Texas
Monday, April 7, 1856, 2 PM

Only Calvin remained on the porch as two riders passed through the front gate. "Daddy, John Watson and Bob Page are here," he called into the house.

"Come inside, son." The visit didn't surprise Woodson. "Mary, this won't be much but keep the kids away from the windows." He added to Luther and Calvin, "Stay between them and your mother and the little ones. Keep your guns in their holsters and your mouths shut." A crisp tone carried his voice as he continued, "Calvin, that means not a word unless they ask you a question and I tell you to answer it. Do we understand one another?"

"Yessir…"

Woodson walked out to the porch and waited.

Watson and Page stopped their horses near where James Callahan and Mallheel Johnson lay. They looked at the dead men before John Watson, the taller man, said, "Well, what I see is what Eli told me we'd find."

Relieved that John wasn't wearing his 'Deputy' star, Woodson asked, "How's Eli?"

"Shot to shit; he has a busted arm and a hole in his neck, but he'll recover."

"Thank God for that! I like Eli, always have," added Woodson. "I reckon James put a lot of pressure on him to come wearing a gun after Eli and I agreed to meet unarmed. Mallheel's boy Thomas, we didn't expect him. That had to be his daddy's doin'."

"You know Thomas' whereabouts? Is he dead?" asked Bob Page.

"If he is, we didn't do it. He shot up the beam over our front window, you can see the bullet holes as plain as day, and then his horse spooked, took off with him holdin' tight. Ain't no tellin' where or how he is."

"Who shot first?" asked Watson.

Woodson held direct eye contact with John Watson. "When James grabbed his gun, we grabbed ours and defended ourselves."

After a look at the slits by the window, John said, "It sounds like you're saying James was dumb enough to draw from an exposed position. Woodson, why would an experienced Ranger like James Callahan do something like that?"

"I can't answer why, but the half dozen bullet holes around the right slit of the window they shot out say what he did."

John dismounted, knelt between James and Mallheel, and examined them. When he looked up, he said, "James' temper wasn't no secret." He shivered while looking at the back of Mallheel's head and frozen smile. "And this son-of-a-bitch would do anything to promote himself. Neither of those is a secret, nor is the character of any of the three of you. As for me, your story and what I see fits. I believe you, Woodson." After a whispered exchange with Bob Page, he continued. "You, me, and Bob all know more people around here admired James than not, and some of them are hot-heads." He nodded toward Woodson, "They'll take vigilante action if I don't do something; Hell, they may take it anyway."

Woodson's voice was soft, somber. "I like to think not. I have to think not, but I agree that there's a chance an angry mob could do what angry mobs do."

"The best and clearest path to avoiding any unlawful acts is the legal one. That means I have to charge you for James and Mallheel's deaths, which I am doing right now. I will testify at that trial and tell the court what I saw today was the aftermath of an act of self-defense. God willing, that will end it. It's the only solution I know with a chance to do that."

Woodson measured his answer before speaking. "I ain't happy but I'm willing to face trial if you support a self-defense plea. People respect you, John. Between your words and me telling the good people of Blanco County the truth, I have no doubt that justice will be served by a fair jury."

"It's our best chance, but nothing is written in stone." John took a deep breath. "I know a lot more about trials and juries, fair and otherwise, than you do, Woodson. Let me share some of what I've learned over the years."

Woodson nodded, listened.

"As a legal matter, you should prevail, but that's only half of the battle. You also have to win the human part of the trial; that's where your life and my reputation will be at stake."

"I ain't for sure what that means," said Woodson.

"First of all, we ain't in Philadelphia. We're in a small town in the Texas Hill Country. Here, unlike in Philadelphia, courts draw juries from a small pool of folks. Here, any jury, even a fair one, reaches a verdict based on if and how events affected them.

Who and what they knew and liked, too. A lot of people around here loved James' gnarly ass, accepted the bad and enjoyed the good. That feeling and a local judge can make witches' brew justice because truth don't mean shit to an emotional angry mob. " He added in a slow, deliberate voice, "I'm not trying to scare you, but I don't want you to face any surprises later."

Woodson rubbed his chin and sighed, "I ain't near as comfortable as I was a few minutes ago. What's the second best and not as clear path to follow? What would you do, John?"

John stepped close to Woodson and spoke in a voice only they could hear. "If we both forget about me arresting you, and I am prepared to do that, you could move to Mexico. After everything James stirred up, these days Rangers are reluctant to cross the river."

Woodson shook his head in a slow almost imperceptible motion. "That's a bleak option, John. If I run, I admit to being guilty of a crime I didn't commit. I did what you and every other man in Blanco County would have done. I, meaning my sons and I, defended our family and home from a hothead with a gun on his hip." Woodson looked south, toward where the Mexican border lay far in the distance and sighed. "And I'm getting old. I ain't strong enough to start over somewhere else."

"I understand." John remounted his horse. "I'll go to the Justice of the Peace and ask for a state appointed judge from Austin. George Lange will do that for me. That'll assure you of a fair trial if a bunch of angry bastards don't decide otherwise."

"I'm obliged, John. What's next?"

"I want you, Calvin, and Mary in protective custody at George Lange's cabin until a jury renders a verdict. You won't be happy, because it'll take a while, but you'll be safe there."

Mary blurted, "We have small children at home…"

"I'll see to it Luther stays home to protect them and Sarah."

Woodson agreed. "Do we go on our own or are you going to take us? When?"

"I'll come for you in a couple hours. Be ready."

NINE

George Lange home and JP Office, Blanco County, Texas
Monday, April 7, 1856, 5 PM

Woodson, Calvin, and Mary stepped onto their front porch when John Watson stopped his horse at the hitching rail. After Calvin nodded a greeting and Mary clasped her hands in front of her stomach, Woodson noted the star pinned to his friend's belt. "That badge is something you didn't bring before."

"Me escorting you, Mary, and Calvin to George Lange's place is official business, and the law requires me to wear it under that circumstance," answered John. "It doesn't show a change in any of my thinking since this morning. When I told you I'd testify yours was an act of self-defense, I meant it, Woodson." He took a breath; seemed to force a smile. "Are you ready?"

Woodson nodded. He felt a sense of relief. "We've packed some clothes and necessities. They're in the living area. Bring the wagon around and let's load up, Calvin."

"Yessir," answered Calvin. He jumped from the porch and started for the barn.

"Let me help," said John, who started to dismount.

"No need, John. We ain't takin' all that much with us."

Five minutes later four travel bags lay in the wagon bed strapped behind the bench seat.

Woodson extended his left hand to Mary. "Let me help you up."

Her quick smile appeared a second before she answered. "I'm half Cherokee. Do you think I need help?" Two quick climbing steps put her on the seat.

Woodson knew an attempt to break tension when he saw one. *My God, what a remarkable woman! She's scared half to death and putting me at ease.* Two steps put him beside Mary on the bench. He took the reins from Calvin. "We'll follow you if that's OK, John?"

George Lange's home, office, and holding facility sat alone just inside the town limits. It was a rough-hewn building, as much a jail or a fort as it was a home and an office. Woodson stepped to the ground and offered Mary his hand. This time she accepted with a soft smile as Calvin walked around the wagon to stand and wait with his parents.

George Lange, a tall mustachioed man with a penchant for eastern dress, soon walked outside. After greeting John for the second time that afternoon, he removed his Bowler hat, and adjusted his horizontal silk necktie and straight tubular trousers. He then addressed the Blasingames. "Woodson, Mrs. Blasingame, Calvin, as I told John this morning, I expect smoke and noise after James' funeral, but that's all. I can handle that easy enough. As you can see, this place is as stout as a bank vault. I assure you, there'll be no lynching."

Everything Woodson saw and George's words painted the same picture. *This place is like a big city bank vault. We could get overrun at home, but not here. John was right. We'll be fine if we get an honest judge.*

Almost as though he'd read Woodson's thoughts, John asked, "Have you wired Austin about getting an impartial judge?"

"I have. I requested the first available of three I trust. Austin will send one of them within the next month or two." George turned to Woodson. "You'll get a fair trial from any of the three. They're the best. There's not a bully in Texas who could crack any of them!"

We're going to survive this. Woodson answered, "That's all we ask…"

"Well, let's be about our business then," answered George. He returned to the door and pushed it open. "Ladies first," he said with a smile. "Mrs. Blasingame, the family's quarters are down the hall behind the first left entryway."

She didn't smile as she answered, "I think you mean the first cell door on the left," while entering.

George's attention turned to Woodson as Calvin entered the building. "Your wife has the gift of defining what she sees, doesn't she?"

Woodson would have laughed if they had been in another place at another time. "She does indeed, George. She does indeed." He followed Calvin into the cell and sat beside Mary before he asked, "Are you going to lock us in here?"

George shook his head from side to side. "Only if you want me to do so." He hung his key ring on a large wood dowel head high on the door's right side. He then added, "Or if I think it will help me keep you from the hands of an angry mob, which is something I do not anticipate."

TEN

Holy Ghost Baptist Church held consecutive funeral services, first for Mallheel Johnson and then for the morning's real focus, James Callahan, on the hottest April day anyone could remember. "Hot as Hell on a stick", one rancher said aloud before his wife squeezed his thigh hard. "Damn, woman!" he hissed.

The preacher leaned over the dais and gripped it as he offered a prayer before beginning the first service. After a following silent moment punctuated by a dozen or more 'amen's', he praised Mallheel's ability to serve the community's need for food and supplies. Personal praises about being clean and well-groomed, and about working hard and honoring his business commitments followed. Nothing else. There were no references to Mallheel's shortcomings, but the congregants, including his widow, remained dry-eyed. The sole exception was his son Thomas. He alone wept, kept the service from being a completely sterile and perfunctory exercise.

The Callahan service followed. Many tears, some real and some false, accented the preacher's golden baritone accounts of James' deeds, noble and heroic acts that Jesus would approve. There was no mention of him murdering aged and infirm Lipan Apache men and women, or of James' forfeited Ranger Star. His wife, Sarah blotted a tear as she took her seat. She sat still, seemed emotionless and quiet, for the rest of the service.

Interments followed in the county's Scot-Irish cemetery. James Callahan met eternity amid a grove of live oak trees atop the cemetery's hill, in the 'honored dead' section. Mallheel Johnson did not.

ELEVEN

George Lange home and JP Office, Blanco County, Texas
Friday, April 11, 1856, 9 AM

Woodson stepped into the hall when he heard John Watson hail George Lange from the outside. "George, it's John Watson. You busy or can I come inside?"

George took an unlit cigar from between his teeth. "Come on in; we're nothing but peace and quiet in here," The wall clock marked nine.

John slapped trail dust from his shirt and pants before entering. "Morning, George." He saw Woodson and asked, "How's George treating you folks, Woodson? Mary and Calvin doing OK?"

"George is a good man. We appreciate how he treats us. He's letting our Sarah or Luther bring us dinner most every evening."

John answered, "I'm not surprised by the treatment, and my guess is Sarah cooks a lot better than George, anyway." He chuckled under his breath while turning to George. "I have a couple of questions for you, and I'm glad Woodson can hear your answers for himself. Preparations for the trial: are they going forward in good order? How about stress, anger, emotions around town?

Have you heard anything I need to know?"

Thank you, John, thought Woodson.

Lange laid the unlit cigar in an ashtray. "As for the first part, Austin says one of our three requested options for a Circuit Judges will be here in early May. I don't know which one or have an exact date yet."

"Good! I take that as good news for justice! How about around town?"

"Everything's peaceful although a few Banty Roosters came by last night. I let them preen and fire a couple rounds in the air before I sent them home. Not much to it."

"They fired three shots," interjected Woodson. "I heard three, but I don't think they hit anything."

George's eyes darted to Woodson and back to John. "Like I said, Banty Roosters."

"How are the Blasingames treating you, George?" asked John.

Woodson knew the question was a signal from John for him to keep quiet. He returned to the family cell and sat beside Mary.

"They're a good family and they do what they can to make my life easy," answered George. "Their Sarah and Luther are attentive; they show it in more ways than just fetching evening meals!" He leaned a little closer and whispered. "That Sarah, if I was twenty years younger..."

John didn't smile. "Forty would be closer than twenty for you." He pointed toward the Blasingame's cell. "I'm going to Lockhart for a few days and want to tell them myself. I don't want them worrying about me or where I am. They have enough to consider already."

"I'll bring them out for you."

George escorted Woodson, Mary, and Calvin to his office area and pointed to chairs lined up near the front door. The Blasin-game's sat. Mary squeezed her husband's hand as John told them he would be in Lockhart for the next three or four days. Woodson patted her knee. "We appreciate you letting us know, John." After a brief pause, he continued in a quiet voice.. "I trust you, John."

TWELVE

George Lange home and JP Office, Blanco County, Texas
Saturday, April 12, 1856, 5PM

George Lange's wall clock sounded five chimes. "That is enough for me. This has been a Hell of a week for a handsome buck of my age," he said aloud before standing. George walked to the hall tree by the front door and felt his coats inside pocket for his cigars and matches. They were there, three or four smokes and at least half a dozen wood matches. He turned toward the doorway leading to the cells. "Woodson," he called, "I am going down to the Boggus for a short while. No sign of any nonsense here or anywhere else, so you folks will be fine. I shall rejoin you in a few hours, more or less."

"Thanks for letting us know, George," answered Woodson.

Lange straightened his tie, put on his jacket, and removed his Bowler from the hall tree. After setting his hat atop his head, he tapped the brim with one finger and smiled at his reflection in the mirror. *How do the local ladies stand it? Lange, you are a handsome Philadelphia gentleman in every way except geography!* He tapped his hat's brim one more time. "Perfect," he said aloud as he opened the door. "I shall lock the door behind me, just to be on the safe side," he called.

"All right,"

The 'click' of the dead bolt sliding into the door frame signaled the Blasingames they were alone.

***

"Do you trust that strutting toad, Woodson?" asked Mary. "I ask because I don't, not much anyway."

Woodson laughed. "Toad or no toad, and with or without trust, Lange won't be a problem for us, Mary. The man I trust is John Watson and I trust him without a doubt. Since John trusted George to extend care and protection to us, I do, too."

Calvin shook his head. "Lange makes me think of those New York sissies that wear the fancy clothes you can read about in the newspaper. What do they call men like that, fops? Something like that, anyway. Bowlers, and top hats, big flat neckties, shiny shoes, and all the prissy rest. None of them look like they could win a fight with a lightnin' bug!" He snickered.

Woodson snapped, "George favors us with his protection, helps us stay alive until the trial, Calvin!" He pointed toward his son. "As for clothes, any man has a right to wear what he wants so long as nobody else has to pay for it! Don't go lookin' for arguments and passing judgement on things that don't concern you, son! Remember the Sermon on the Mount!"

Calvin mimicked the Preacher's baritone voice. "Do unto others as you would have them do unto you." He offered a brief laugh before sighing, "I know you're right, Papa. My weakness is that I'm not as confident as I was when we came in here." He took a deep breath and shook his head. "Fact is, although I know everything you said is right, my gut fears you ain't."

Woodson answered, "Your gut will get past that fear if you start your every thought about George Lange with two certainties. One, he is bound by the law and his word to John Watson to keep us safe and two, he ain't spending our money. George may not be the kind of fellow either of us would want to hunt or drink with, but our concerns have more to do with the service he's honor bound to provide us; service that has nothing to do with hunting or drinking."

Calvin leaned back, rested his head on the cool stone and live oak wall behind him, and closed his eyes.

Mary touched her son's knee and looked at her husband. "I love you, Woodson."

"And I love you, too, Mary. We'll be fine. I promise you that." He walked into the hallway and then to George's front office. He looked through each window and listened for any out of place sound. Nothing. All of nature lay quiet.

THIRTEEN

Boggus Saloon, Blanco County Texas
Saturday, April 12, 1856, 6PM

A slight chill raced down George's spine as he looped his horse's reins around the hitching rail and slapped some non-existent dust from his jacket and pants. *Touch of winter; it is not gone yet,* He forgot about the cool air as he entered the town's main Saloon, where heat and smell dominated everything. The dimly lit bar was defined by its warmth and odors, a mix of sweet cheap perfumes, and sour unbathed bodies. Although he would prefer an emporium cleaner and with a better aroma, George accepted Boggus for what it was. The Boggus provided him two of life's most basic needs with no mess to clean up later. There he drank his fill of numbing alcohol and purchased female companionship when he chose.

True to its mien, the Boggus straight backed chairs circled dark brown scarred tables and a row of gas lights illuminated scratched mirrors behind the bar. On the floor, sawdust kept the sounds of men walking on the discolored pine floor low. It was a cushioning no longer needed by the long unused piano facing the wall across from the bar. All the white keys were gone.

"Ah," George murmured. His favorite table, the one in the corner between the bar and the front window, was available. As soon as he sat and laid his Bowler on the table, a bar girl in a low-cut flouncy orange dress cinched tight at the waist all but danced to his table.

Under long eye lashes and rouged cheeks, she blew George a kiss and said in a pouting voice, "I haven't seen you in a while, Georgie! I was afraid you were mad at me!"

"How could a gentleman such as I ever feel anger for the magnificent Miss Cleopatra Goodbody?" He smiled when she took a deep breath and pushed her breasts forward.

"Would you like something special tonight? I so hope so, dear Georgie!" She leaned toward him to allow her high and round breasts to present themselves anew and not-quite concealed by the neckline of her orange dress.

"Absolutely, but first bring me a cold beer and a bottle of Rye Whisky. Oh, and Cleo, make sure my glass is a clean one!"

"Anything for you!"

George winked and smiled before she walked away. He thought about her last name; he hadn't done that in a while. Cleopatra Goodbody! Nobody had a name like Cleopatra Goodbody! At one time he had wondered what her real name was, but it didn't matter anymore. For his purposes, be it bringing him beer and whiskey or rolling with him upstairs, Cleopatra Goodbody was as good a name as any. His smile broadened.

The smile ended when Eamon Cox surprised George by sitting down beside him. Eamon was large, an unkempt bearded man in his thirties with arms the size of George's thighs and long, thin ringlets of oily hair.

George hid the fear that grabbed his stomach. "Can I buy you a drink, Eamon, a beer or something?" He had never spoken to Eamon, but knew of him, of his bad temper anyway, as did most people in Blanco County.

Eamon grinned. He stuck his tongue through his teeth where his left canine once was, and answered, "Yup! I'll have a beer!"

His breath stunk so bad it almost made George sick. Its smell outdid both the Saloon's reputation and Eamon's own. George shifted his chair a few inches to the right and began breathing through his mouth to dull his sense of smell before raising two fingers to Cleo, who was laughing with the bartender, for two beers. She brought them and left without comment.

George sipped his beer and watched Eamon drain half of his before he asked, "So, Eamon, we talk at last. To what do I owe the pleasure of this first conversation?"

Eamon finished his beer. "Another," he said after resting his mug on the table. George signaled for two more.

When Cleo brought the mugs of beer, George said, "Both are for Eamon." She set them down and hurried from the table.

George leaned forward as Eamon drained half a mug. "Eamon, what say you? The floor is yours."

Eamon belched and wiped his mouth. "Blasingame. I hear you got him, his squaw, and his boy Calvin at your place." He finished the second mug.

George sipped his beer before he answered. "That is correct. They are in protective custody. That will remain the case until they are tried for their roles in the killings of James Callahan and Mallheel Johnson."

"I did some work for Callahan, and he paid me for it. I need that money to help take care of my wife and children. Can't provide all they need without it. Who's gonna pay me now?" Eamon drank half of his third beer. "Blasingame put an end to it. I figure he owes me."

"That sounds like a question for the courts to answer, Eamon. I suggest you have an attorney look into the matter for you." George took another sip. *God, get this animal away from my table!*

Eamon shook his head. "Ain't got enough cash on hand to pay no attorney, lawyer, whatever. Them guys don't work for nothing. What's plain as day is Blasingame took my ongoing money away when he killed the man what give it to me. That makes him responsible, and I intend to get what's mine from Woodson." He reached across the table and gripped George's forearm. "No son-of-a-bitch can hurt my family and get away with it." Eamon released George's arm and leaned back in his chair.

George decided his immediate fate lay in his ability to present himself with some of the theatre skills, techniques that pushed fear from his mind and voice, he learned as part of the Baltimore Players Group. He took a breath, shook his head, and stepped into character. He became Lear after betrayal by Goneril and Regan. Sad and angry, he sneered, "You are wrong. You can't see the truth. Woodson Blasingame doesn't have any money, Eamon. He's a hard-working man, but he's short for cash, like almost everybody else in Blanco County. It's just not there."

"Then I'll take it out of his ass," answered Eamon. He drained the last half of his third beer.

High drama is way over his head, thought George. *Maybe humor.* He tried Puck from Midsummer Night's Dream. "Want another?" he asked in an impish voice after tapping his fingers on the table.

"No." Eamon wiped his mouth with anger in his eyes.

So much for the Baltimore Players…God, help me, please!

"They's a lot of people around here who want to skin Blasingame for what he done. It ain't just me, it's a lot of men! Some of them are mad enough to come with me when I collect my money next Monday at sundown." He grabbed George's forearm again. This time he squeezed a bit harder as he leaned forward and whispered, "If my money ain't there, I'll get my friends to help me kill both Woodson and his worthless son. It'll be blood or money for the Blasingames." George tried to pull his arm away without being too conspicuous. Eamon had none of it. He held tight, gripped a little harder, as he continued, "We'll kill you, too, if you get in our way. You understand?" Eamon released George's arm and stood. "It'll be money or death Monday at sundown. There ain't no other options. Lange. You didn't answer when I asked if you understood! Say it now! Do you?" When George nodded, Eamon said, "Thanks for the beers," and left the saloon without another word.

Cleo returned to the table. "George, you're as white as a ghost. What was that about?"

"Nothing good, my dear," he answered in a soft voice. "Nothing good at all." He took a deep breath. "And as for tonight's dalliance, I must ask that we postpone it until a later date." He handed her a two-dollar gold piece. "Pay for the beers out of that and keep the rest for yourself. I feel it's both the most and the least I can do tonight." Neither George Lange nor Cleopatra Goodbody said another word to each other as he left the saloon.

FOURTEEN

George Lange home and JP Office, Blanco County, Texas
Saturday, April 12, 1856, 8 PM

Woodson looked up when he heard the dead bolt lock retreat from the door frame. When the door creaked open, he took a step toward the cell door. "George, is that you?"

"It is I." The voice seemed flat, less than human and disassociated from the man using it.

Woodson walked to the door leading from the office to the cells as George closed and relatched the deadbolt. "You weren't gone as long as we thought. Are you feeling all right, George? Ain't none of my business, but you look a little washed out if you don't mind me saying."

George didn't answer as he lay his Bowler on the hall tree's top peg. He looked into the wall mirror behind it. *I do look like I saw a ghost. Hell, anybody would after an experience like that.* He shook his head from side to side and tugged at his jacket. He then straightened his pants and slapped nonexistent dust from them as his mind raced *My God, what shall I do?*

Mary walked to Woodson side. There she stared at George as

Woodson tried to make a joke. "Was the music a little to loud for your ear?"

"Not a problem since someone made off with the piano's Ivory keys." George almost grinned. "You need to get out more, Woodson." He and Woodson shared a brief laugh. Mary didn't join them. Instead, she stared at George's face, eyes. George glanced at her and returned his attention to Woodson. "I am exhausted," he said as he began walking toward the door to his desk's left. "I will be in here should anything requiring my attention arise, but as I said earlier, all is quiet. I intend to read for a while and get a good night's sleep." He smiled. It was a large, beaming smile. "See you in the morning!" He entered his quarters, closed the door behind him, and latched it.

"I reckon George drank too much beer in too short a time. That'll make you sick for sure, and he's got that pasty look about him," said Woodson.

"Beer isn't George Lange's pasty look problem tonight," answered Mary.

The remark confused Woodson. "Then what?" he asked.

Mary didn't smile. "I don't know, but he didn't look like he'd been drinking, not much, anyway." She walked toward their cell. "It'll come to me," she added without looking back as she continued to the bench seat.

Woodson sat beside her. "What's with George?" He tried to make a small joke. "That Cherokee blood tryin' to tell you something?"

She patted her husband's knee. "I guess we've been in here long enough for me to look for things to worry about."

Across the room, Calvin began to snore. "It's early, but maybe we should turn in, too."

She nodded, squeezed Woodson's knee, and released it. "At least Calvin doesn't let this mess keep him awake at night."

"Nothing keeps that boy awake!"

FIFTEEN

George Lange home and JP Office, Blanco County, Texas
Sunday, April 13, 1856, 9 AM

"I hear the wagon," said Woodson. "Luther and Sarah must be here." He, Mary, and Calvin entered the office area, where he unlatched the deadbolt and opened the door as Luther lead Sarah, complete with a breakfast basket, through the front door.

As they exchanged hugs, kisses, and greetings, George Lange joined them from his quarters. After shaking Luther's hand, he bowed to Sarah. "Ah, the lovely and talented Miss Blasingame!" He kissed her hand, and added, "Welcome to my humble abode!"

Sarah handed Luther the basket. "I brought a full Sunday breakfast for Momma, Papa, and Calvin. There's plenty for us all, if you'd like to join us, Mister Lange."

Woodson knew why Sarah had called George Lange 'Mister' instead of George. *That's my girl!* he thought.

George declined the invitation saying he was to join his sister and her husband this morning. He added, "Woodson, Mary. I should be back by midafternoon. As all remains calm around here, I don't anticipate any difficulties." He leaned toward Sarah and kissed her cheek. It was a light peck. "Miss Sarah, I hope you and Luther enjoy your visit today."

She didn't respond to George's cheek kiss. "Thank you, Mister Lange. I'm sure we will."

He went to the hall tree, removed his Bowler, and set it just-so on his head. After a quick tap confirmed to all it was in place, he touched the front doorknob. "Good morning to all!" he said as he left the building.

Sarah and Mary spread a tablecloth over George's desk and the Blasingames shared conversation, a blend of serious and humorous thoughts, and a full meal for over an hour.

As Sarah and Mary packed their bowls, dishes, silverware, and tablecloth in the basket, Luther said, "Papa, when Mister Lange was on the way out, he said everything's calm around here and he didn't expect any difficulties. That ain't what I heard when Herr Maassen in the German area came by last night about nine o'clock."

"Late for a visit, even on a Saturday," said Woodson.

"I wasn't expecting him, but we'd talked before about us trading him some turkeys for one of his hogs. Anyhow, we got to talking. That's when he told me different from Lange's account about no difficulties."

Mary and Sarah stopped packing. Woodson absorbed Luther's words before he asked, "What kind and who from?"

Sarah covered her eyes. Mary put her arms around her daughter as Luther continued, "Eamon Cox for one. Maassen makes and sells German style beer to Boggus, and he delivered a keg between seven and eight last night. That's late, too, but you know them Germans. They work long days."

"What did he see or hear?"

"He saw Eamon talking to George Lange. Heard him, too. You know how loud Eamon can be and when he drinks, he gets even louder. Herr Maassen said he was talking tough, talking about getting you about Callahan. He told Lange him and his friends were coming over here to get money or you and Calvin. He said they'd kill you both."

"What did George do? Did he say anything?"

Luther shook his head. "He didn't say a damned thing. Just sat there like he was scared shitless!"

"Eamon can do that to a normal sized man," answered Woodson. "Another fact is that Eamon never lets the truth get in the way of a good story and gets worse when he gets a snootful, too."

Luther pointed to the front door. "We gotta get you, Momma, and Calvin out of here! You can hide out for a while, maybe a year, and let this blow over."

Woodson shook his head. "Son, there are a lot of things at play here. One is that Calvin and I are charged with murder. That will never go away. Another is that if we stay here and stand trial, we will win. We'll be acquitted. That's a fact. Third, anything Eamon tells you, mad, drunk, both, and otherwise, is likely nonsense. He doesn't think ahead. He can't! It all comes down to us staying and winning. Eamon Cox's big mouth won't play a role in that. He can't play a role in anything that doesn't involve getting an ox out of a ditch. Hell, he can't even tell you what he ate for supper last night!"

"Momma, Calvin..." pled Luther.

"Your Father is right, Luther. We stay," answered Mary. Sarah buried her head in her mother's neck without speaking.

Calvin didn't speak either. He nodded his agreement to his mother's words.

SIXTEEN

George Lange home and JP Office, Blanco County, Texas
Monday, April 14, 1856, 6 PM

George left the front door open as he stepped out on the porch, struck a match on his boot, and lit a fresh cigar. After two puffs and a smoke ring, he sat in a chair behind his hitching rail. He stared into the night but saw nothing. It could have been a peaceful time, a good cigar under a clear sky in temperate weather, but fearful worries wouldn't allow it. Dark intimidating thoughts created a profound concern for his future, his reputation, indeed his life, and left no room for anything else. George tipped the ash from his cigar. He sighed, fed on unprovoked worries, and lived fears both real and imaginary until a series of torches and unknown out-of-place sounds accompanying sporadic gunshots pierced the silence.

He pulled the ember from the tip of his cigar and crushed it in the dirt beside the step up to the porch. *Torches and voices, male voices, occasional pistol fire, coming this way from town,* George thought. *That has to be trouble brewing if ever I saw it!* He tucked his remaining cigar in his jacket pocket and returned inside. He closed and latched the door and took his holster from the peg behind the hall tree. It was a short walk from there to the cells area, where he met interested stares from all three Blasingames. George buckled his holster and tied it to his right leg with a leather lace.

George's skin looked pasty to Mary. She said, "Somebody's shooting pistols and hollerin' out there, George. What's going on? Tell me what I'm hearing." She asked. "Is a mob heading this way?"

He stared at the wall over the Blasingame's heads rather than making eye contact with any of them as he answered, "A few drunks acting out it looks to me: nothing new about that. I can run them off easy enough."

"My hearing isn't as good as Mary's," said Woodson, "But the gunshots and screaming I heard didn't come from a 'few' of anything, drunk or otherwise, George. It sounds like a full-grown mob." He extended his right hand. "Give Calvin and me our side-arms, our rifles, too, for just in case. We won't use them except to defend ourselves should the need arise, and we'll give them back to you when the threats gone. If you're right, if they're just 'A few drunks acting out' nobody will know, we'll be obliged to you, and it won't make a penny's worth of difference to anybody else."

"That would make me a law breaker." George shook his head from side to side in two quick jerky motions. "Texas law says 'no' to arming anyone incarcerated under my jurisdiction, under my supervision, for any reason. That is that. Austin writes the rules and I follow them, end of discussion. Besides, as I said, I can handle unruly drunks with ease. I assure you; you all are safe, secure. Trust me."

Mary sighed, "They sound unruly, loud, with a lust for Blasingame blood."

Calvin said, "Mama's right, George, and what I hear says they's more of them than you have bullets in that Colt, a lot more. If they rush you, they can take you out. If that happens, we'll have no way to save ourselves. I'm not saying you'd be afraid of them. What I'm saying is look at their numbers. All of us can hold them off. One of us can't."

George tugged at his vest. *God, I hate it when uneducated dolts take it upon themselves to lecture me. About anything!* After brushing dust from his pants, he spoke with a stern voice. "This conversation is at an end. I will act as the law defines my duty, no more and no less. All you Blasingames have to do is just stay where you are and relax." A faux smile appeared. "As I said, trust me." Without another word, he left the cell area, closed its door, and returned to the porch chair behind the hitching rail.

SEVENTEEN

George Lange home and JP Office, Blanco County, Texas
Monday, April 14, 1856, 7PM

George's worries walked on his skin when he looked toward town. *They were right. This looks worse than I thought.* Two hundred yards in the distance, he squinted while counting a dozen torches and heard the early distant sound of perhaps thirty riders heading his way. He pulled his part-smoked cigar from his jacket pocket and relit it. Two strong puffs later, he admired his smoke's bright red ember. *They all have to be armed,* he thought. He spoke aloud, but in a soft voice, "At least twenty-five, maybe thirty, armed men heading this way under a dozen torches." He measured the situation. "At least one of them has the brain power and disposition of a Baltimore Harbor wharf rat." His skin dampened before growing cold and dry. *"And I have six shots and the promise of a nice funeral."* He snickered. His quick laugh did nothing to abate reality as the riders drew closer. *They look rough, like they want trouble,* George thought as they stopped their horses, fifteen to a side, behind the hitching rails on either side of the JP Office steps. No one dismounted; they sat as though awaiting instruction.

George knew if he was to control the group, he would have to take charge right away. His porch chair squeaked as he stood. *Back to the Shakespeare Ensemble and the Baltimore Players Group! Use those skills and look resolute and just tough enough. Don't let them know how scared you are,* George told himself. He stood erect, as tall as he could, and pulled the right side of his jacket behind his holster. In measured and manful strides, he walked to the steps and made eye contact with half of the riders, showing no fear as he did so. The intoxicating smell of the greasepaint so many years before flooded him as he raised both hands, a signal to the riders for quiet.

Astride his horse near the steps, Eamon Cox understood but ignored the gesture. "We ain't making no noise and we ain't here to watch you strut around the porch, Lange." He swung his right leg over his saddle and jumped to the ground. Every eye, both George's and the vigilante's, watched him climb to the JP Office porch with casual strides.

The whole of this is almost too casual, thought George. It's as though *Eamon and the others are in a choreographed scene. As if they are the performers instead of me.* A fear spasm traveled down his spine.

Eamon stepped close enough for George to smell his beer-soaked breath. *Oh great! He loaded up with beer before coming. I dare not show fear.*

Eamon hissed a command. "You know why me and my friends are here. Save your ass, George. Give me the key and get out of the way."

George felt his legs weaken. *Distraction! Dear God, I need distraction!* He puffed out his chest under and created a faux smile. "What say we call it a day and head down to Boggus for a few beers, Eamon? My treat! A free beer for each of your friends and all you want for yourself. I shall join you."

"Buying a couple beers at Boggus don't make us friends, Lange. Don't lie to me about not rememberin' what I told you what was gonna happen tonight if I didn't have my money."

"Eamon, I...", traced a path across George's lips.

Eamon laid both hands on George's chest and pushed hard. Lange stumbled three steps back before he tripped and fell into the door jamb. He slid down it, landed with a hard thud that didn't keep him down or out of character. With nothing to lose, he jumped to his feet and became Iago the deceitful self-absorbed manipulator in Othello. He pointed a finger at Eamon. "Are you aware I am trying to help you, Eamon? If I am to be the aide you need in your quest, you will keep your hands to yourself! Cut out the pushing, all of the bully nonsense, and let me save an effort that is off to a bad start!"

Eamon fell quiet. He and the few vigilantes that talked among themselves seemed confused.

To George's great relief, none struck an aggressive posture. He knew the seeming confusion and general silence were his cues to take control. He put his hands on his hips, a pose that proclaimed authority, and said to the mob, "All of you, think about who owes me favors before you abuse my authority physically or emotional-ly. I warn you. Do not play rough with me!" He ran his right index finger down the complete line of mounted horsemen. "If you do, and/or I tell men capable of killing you one and all for any reason, you all will die!" George's bravado penetrated the riders, and the fear that drained from his spine flowed into most of the mob's. *As good as I have ever been!* thought George.

The muted rumblings from the riders announced that George

had achieved what he needed most, but the comfort control gave him proved short-lived and illusory. Eamon and a few vigilantes didn't share the fear George seeded in the mob behind the hitching rail. Eamon spat in the dirt. His eyes seemed to glow as he said, "I see what you're doing, you slick talking son-of-a-bitch! You think I'm stupid! Well, I ain't stupid! None of us are stupid except you!" He walked to George, gripped the JP's arm., and began to squeeze, to tighten his grip. When his lock on George's arm was harder than in the Saloon, he spoke in a voice loud enough for his mob to hear. "You gon' die tonight. You gon' die right here, you pig shit son-of-a-bitch! Talkin' to me, to us, like we're stupid ain't gonna make you anything but dead. From now on, you do what I say when I say it, or I kill you on the spot! That includes right here and now. I want you to get your ass the Hell away from here right now! Do you understand me?"

"I understand," whispered George.

Eamon squeezed harder; his grip felt like a vise clamping George's arm, making it grow numb. "Say it louder;" ordered Eamon. "Say everything you understand loud and clear!"

"I understand that I am going to do what you say when you say it and that includes leaving my office now," George announced. His voice was loud enough for everyone along the hitching rails to hear. Eamon released George's arm.

George's mind raced as he moved his numb arm back and forth to promote blood circulation. *The Blasingames are done for! Get back in character, get out of here, and save your life, Lange!*

Most of a minute passed before Eamon asked in a voice loud and clear, "Why you still here, Georgie?" He exchanged grins with some of his vigilantes. "Make up your mind. Are you staying here and dying or leaving and living? Say it! Are you gon' live or die?"

George ignored the obvious insult being addressed as a child, a young George, and stayed in character as best he could. He knew doing so would keep from having to confront Eamon Cox and his cowardice and dereliction of duty. "I choose to live. I shall exercise my choice by leaving the premises; a departure in which I know nothing of you, Eamon, nor your colleagues, nor your shared intent." George tried to concentrate on the pride he felt because he wasn't crying and that his voice hadn't cracked. He turned to Eamon and forced a humorless smile. His voice was flat, emotionless, as he asked, "I need enough time to establish my presence elsewhere before you proceed? May I have an hour or two? I need that to protect myself from a charge of complicit behavior."

Eamon's voice sounded calm as he answered. "I don't know what complicit means, but we'll give you at least an hour, maybe a little more, if you get your ass out of here right now."

The tone of Eamon's voice eased some of George's fears. "Thank you. My mare is in the stable, second stall on the right. Will someone retrieve her from the stable and saddle her for me?"

Eamon pointed to the two men nearest the stable. "Get his horse and bring it to the steps." An owl's hoot in the distance broke the following silence, but no one near or on the porch spoke as the men walked to the stable. Ten minutes later, they returned with George's saddled horse and draped her reins over the rail near the steps.

Eamon waved his left arm to the left and then to the right, a signal to his vigilantes to separate. They did so. The path between them gave George free access to the road behind them.

Pasty and struggling to keep his emotions under control, George stepped from the porch to the hard dry earth below it. He held his horse's reins in one hand as he turned and looked back

In an anguished voice, he issued a one word plea. "Eamon..." His voice faded into the silence that surrounded him and the mob.

"Git!" said Eamon. His voice was strong, threatening.

George stuck his left foot in its stirrup, gripped his saddle horn, and pulled himself into his saddle. Still in character, still fighting the shame he felt, George sought a justifying shard of dignity for his criminal cowardice. "Let everyone among you know," he said in a soft voice that was loud enough for all to hear, "I owed James Callahan." He turned his horse's head toward town and spoke louder as he added, "James, we're even now." George then looked at Eamon and made a last request. "I think our Ranger friend would appreciate you lettin' Mrs. Mary go. It's common knowledge she is part Indian, but she is no Lipan Apache, and most of the time James respected women."

Eamon nodded.

George touched his heels to his mare's flanks. She whinnied once as he turned her toward the saloon.

EIGHTEEN

George Lange home and JP Office, Blanco County, Texas
Monday, April 14, 1856, 7:30PM

Woodson felt the silence as much as he heard it, the lack of gar-
bled hard-edged words outside that no longer echoed into the
back room. He glanced at Mary without speaking. *Where the Hell
is George?*

"Pa," said Calvin, "None of them voices sounded right. They
were angry for the most part, like they was up to something. Now
I don't hear anything. The quiet makes me wonder more than
when they were strutting, showing off..."

"I understand.," answered Woodson. "What I've seen in life
tells me that a mob talkin' ain't a mob doin'. We don't know what's
going on out there so let's don't jump to any conclusions, but I
agree about the quiet. It makes me curious if nothing else." He
thought for a second. "Grab the cell key from the hook by the door
so we can lock ourselves in here for safety if the need arises."
Mary folded her arms. He soothed her in gentle tones. "That's a
'just in case.' Don't go borrowing trouble. I'm sure George will be
in here in a minute to tell us what happened."

Calvin slid his hand along the wall by the cell. He touched the hook and felt for the cell key. It wasn't there. He went to the door and tugged. The door was locked. "Pa, no key on the hook and the cell door is locked. We're trapped. We got no guns, a locked door, and no key!"

"What am I borrowing now?" asked Mary, while patting her husband's knee.

Woodson didn't answer. He crossed the cell and tested the door for himself. Locked. He then walked to the front corner and felt the hook. The key wasn't there. "Calvin, check the bars on the window."

Calvin did so. "Stout," he answered while shaking his head. "I can't wiggle any of them, much less make them turn. They ain't goin' nowhere in that adobe. The only way out of here is through that locked door and we ain't got the key."

NINETEEN

Boggus Saloon, Blanco County, Texas
Monday, April 14, 1856, 7:45 PM

A canopy of silence surrounded horse and rider during the ride to town. On the surface, all seemed quiet, peaceful, almost serene. George felt neither peace nor serenity as he bowed his head and closed his eyes while entering Blanco County's business area. *Those damned vigilantes know what a coward I am now. No Shakespearean persona could hide the fact that I left a family under my care to die at their hand! Not even so much as a defying word from you, you gutless son-of-a-bitch! A real man would have stood up! Would have stood up to Eamon in the Saloon! Would have stood up to him and his louts again tonight! But you, George Lange, are not a real man! You are what you are and always have been. You are a mewling toad of a man, a man unworthy of life itself and afraid to fight, die if need be, and willing to stand up for what is right.* He said aloud to no one, "God forgive me for what I am, but I'm not going to ride back there and die to justify my sorry existence."

Fifteen minutes later George stopped at the Boggus hitching

rail as near the doorway as possible. His horse was a known commodity around town, and he wanted her seen. He dismounted, looped his reins over the rail twice, and stepped up to the Saloon's porch. "Here I shall drink for hours and if I am capable, forget about this horrible evening in the comfort of Miss Cleopatra Goodbody's arms." He entered through the swinging doors. "Good," he said aloud. His regular table was unoccupied. George walked across the sawdust strewn floor, through the sweat and cheap perfume that hung in the air, and chose a chair at his table that faced the bar. He caught Cleopatra's eye. She smiled and blew him a kiss.

"Sweet Jesus!" George thought *I run from justice and hide from my self-loathing behind a fallen woman!* His mind raced. *What is the value of a man whose only pleasure in life lies in the arms and smile of a prostitute; a woman who, truth told, adores the gold I provide her and nothing more.*

Two men he did not know looked up as George muttered, "Alas, I am nothing save one of the lovely and licentious Miss Goodbody's temporary procurement tools. I am a male who rents her body but cannot touch her soul."

Cleo brought a welcoming smile and flirty steps under her orange flouncy dress to his table. "Beer and a bottle or just beer, Georgie? And I am so happy to see you!"

"Beer and a bottle of Rye, Cleo. Perhaps a little time later, too?"

She giggled as she leaned over the table and teased his chin with her right index finger.

"The view remains remarkable," George forced a smile. *And God knows you are a woman who can build a fire on the wettest day since Noah's ark!*

"Anything for you, Georgie," she whispered while fluttering her eyelashes. She stood up straight and rested her hands on her hips. "Including the cleanest beer and whiskey glasses I can find!" She giggled again and swished back to the bar. Less than a minute later, while waiting for George's beer and Rye. Cleo blew a kiss to a stranger entering the saloon.

A new business acquaintance, no doubt. George sighed and the men at the next table looked up again as he said, "A woman whose real name I do not know, a woman who trades me and others sex for money provides the only joy my miserable life affords me." Oblivious to the stares his words drew, George shook his head. *What are you now, George? You are as much Eamon Cox's cowardly whore as Cleopatra Goodbody is for any man with a few pieces of gold.* Dear God, what have I become,"

One cowboy at the next table whispered to his friend, "Bastard's crazy." His friend nodded. Neither looked George's way again.

TWENTY

George Lange home and JP Office, Blanco County, Texas
Monday, April 14, 1856, 8 PM

The doorway separating the cells from the office swung open hard and fast. It sped through its arc and slammed against with wall with a wood-splintering crash. A tall man with a dreadlocked beard that clung to dried tobacco juice stepped into the cells area and wrapped his hands around iron bars.

"What the Hell are you doing here drunk as a skunk, Leonard?" asked Woodson.

In a voice pitched an octave too high, Leonard Jacks all but slurred, "I'm here on personal business. We all here on personal business." He snorted. "I hear you said Miz Mary was borrowin' trouble. She ain't borrowin' nothin'; the trouble for you, your wife, and all the Blasingames is right here and of your making." He released the iron bars, seemed to take a misstep, and then gripped them again, tighter this time.

"Crazy drunk bastard," said Calvin as he stood. He snarled, "That's you I'm callin' a crazy drunk bastard, Jacks!" and took two quick steps toward the bars before Woodson grabbed his shoulder.

"Stop," barked Woodson. He released his son's shoulder and pointed to the bench seat beside Mary. "Sit down and keep your mouth shut."

Calvin nodded but didn't answer. He sat where his father said and folded his arms across his chest.

Woodson's attention returned to Leonard Jacks who held the bars with a tight grip. Woodson inhaled enough air for a deep breath. His mind raced. *Not only do I smell rotgut whisky on that son-of-a-bitch's breath, his face looks like he's been sucking it down for hours. The way he grabs and turns loose of those bars says he's whatever comes after drunk, and that ain't a good sign.*

The rumbling and angry voices of thirty men who came with Eamon Cox sounded through the door to the office. They fell silent as Eamon cox passed through them and paused in the cell area doorway.

Woodson measured Eamon as they made eye contact. Amid a heavy silence, Eamon offered a grin that showed no humor and pulled a key from his pants' pocket. He held it over his head and shook it. "This here is for your door, c'ept it's our door now on accounta we got the key!" He chuckled, tossed the key from one hand to the other and back, and waved it in the air. Eamon snorted another chuckle. It held no more humor than before, less if possible; this one sounded dry, empty, bereft of humanity.

Woodson caught the change of tone. He turned to Calvin and mouthed, "Drunk. Probably drunk and mean."

Eamon made a shooing motion with his right hand. "Move," he said to the drunk man holding the cell bars. The man took two steps to his right and kept one hand on a cell bar as he did so. Eamon approached the cell door, held a door bar with his left hand and tugged twice. Nothing happened. The door remained locked. He inserted the key into the lock with his right hand. A single dull clicking sound of metal linking with metal filled the cell. Eamon took his hand from the key and said through the still locked door, "I come for my money. Hand it over or else."

"We all come for our money you took from us when you killed James Callahan," said a voice behind Eamon.

"We are under the supervision of the Blanco County Court and you are breaking the law just by being here." A strong silence followed. "Where's George?" asked Woodson. "You do something to him?"

"He ain't here."

"Is he dead?"

"Not unless his whore screwed him to death," said Eamon. The crowd standing behind him roared with laughter.

Woodson asked, "You buy him off? With what?"

"Not money! You got our money! I scared him off is more like it." The crowd roared again. Eamon's voice turned cold again. "The talking has ended. My money, our money, pay up!" He and Woodson locked stares; neither man blinked as Eamon tugged at the cell door. Locked. He turned the key. Two quick clicks. "Oops," said Eamon. "Looks like your door ain't locked no more." He made a sound that mixed a laugh and a giggle, but it held no sense of humor, no relief, as he pulled the door an inch from the lock. As Eamon ran a finger down the line separating the door from the cell, he said, "You ain't got enough in the game to cooperate, yet Blasingame!" He opened the cell door wide enough for a man to pass through. "I'm gonna change that." He waved, it was a calling wave, to Leonard, who still held the bars beside him, "The woman, Blasingame's half-breed squaw. Her white name is Mary. That's what they call her, anyway. Go in there and fetch her to me. Drag her ass out here if she don't cooperate!" Eamon wiped his mouth on his left sleeve. "I don't want to bloody up or hurt no woman, not even a squaw, but sooner or later, Mary here will convince Woodson to do the right thing!" Eamon's smile returned for an instant before it faded away. "Ain't never killed a woman. Yet, anyway, Woodson."

Woodson stepped between Mary and the wiry-bearded Leonard Jacks entering the cell. Calvin stood; two steps forward put him at his father's left side. Three feet lay between Woodson and Leonard's immediate threat to Mary, but Eamon, now a mere three feet behind Leonard, was the darker and more formidable threat to his wife.

First things first thought Woodson. His attention returned to Leonard Jacks, and he linked eyes and Leonard with a cold and harsh stare. Woodson saw fear. *He's scared. Scared of me? Yes. Scared of being embarrassed in front of his friends. Yes, that, too.*

A brief look over his left shoulder seemed to push the wiry Leonard Jacks into action. He stepped left to get around Woodson.

Woodson stepped to his right, blocked Leonard's path, and laid a gentle hand on the man's chest. Woodson's voice was soft, confident, and hard to hear more than a foot away. "You don't want any of me and we both know it, don't we Leonard? We both know I can cripple your ass for life before Eamon could get here and help you. Don't we, Leonard? Am I right? Do I have to prove it?"

"Blasingame, you need to step aside." Jack's voice was soft, no louder than Woodson's, but the timbre was wrong. He didn't sound like the brave vigilante, he sounded like the terrified one, the trapped one.

Behind Jacks, Eamon Cox gripped the cell door with both hands. He shouted, "Dammit to Hell, Leonard! Do what I said or get the Hell out of the way!"

Leonard Jacks' voice sounded like a prayer without prayerful words. "If you got the money, hand it to Eamon, Woodson. Otherwise, bad things are gonna happen to all you Blasingames and you and me both know it."

Eamon entered the cell, pushed Leonard into Calvin, and started toward Mary. Woodson laid his left hand flat, extended his left elbow, and swung his hand in a flat, fast arc toward Eamon Cox's throat. The blow landed hard, its full force making a 'thud' sound as it struck Eamon's Adams Apple. As Eamon grabbed his throat with both hands and gasped for air, Woodson kicked the big man's crotch with his right boot. Eamon collapsed and mouthed airless screams as Woodson kicked him three times more. Four rough hands pushed Woodson off Eamon, a series of kicks and blows to the head drove him against the wall and then to the floor. Woodson's eyes, blurred by blood and tears, gave him a distorted view of Leonard Jacks and two of his fellow vigilantes. The new pair began to maul Mary. They first grabbed her hair, then locked their arms around her arms and waist, and pinned her arms behind her. She kicked Leonard in the stomach and bit the closest vigilante, Junior Abbot, who was the larger of the two maulers. Junior cursed Mary and slapped her across the mouth hard enough to draw blood. Junior wiped her spittle from his mouth and cheeks before wrapping his right arm around Mary's neck. He began squeezing air, and life, from her body.

Woodson struggled to the path between the cells, trying to reach her, but the cold reality of a vigilante's gun barrel touching Mary's forehead and a shouted "I'll kill her if you don't stop, Woodson!" ended his attempt.

"All right," said Woodson. The vigilante loosened his grip on

Mary's throat. As she panted, gasped for air, a second commotion tore away part of everyone's attention. It was the mob mauling the uncooperative Calvin.

Woodson moved closer to Mary. She pulled a hand free and grabbed his shirt to no avail. The vigilantes separated her from her husband and shoved them both through the front door and down the steps from the front porch. A hard push left Calvin sprawled beneath his parents.

<h1 style="text-align:center">TWENTY-ONE</h1>

**Outside, George Lange home and JP Office, Blanco
County, Texas
Monday, April 14, 1856, 8:30 PM**

Eamon Cox, who now walked in short choppy steps and spoke in a raspy voice stepped into the JP Office's doorway. "Line 'em up, all three of em, and tie their hands to the hitching rail behind their backs.

The exhausted family no longer could resist. They stood along the rail, facing the road with their hands behind them, as a killing arc of vigilantes formed in the road. As it tightened, animal-like howls erupted as the masked men kicked Woodson's and Calvin's legs until neither could stand. Leonard Jacks and two other men bullied Mary, grabbing her breasts, and twisting them hard. They wanted to make her cry. They failed. She did not respond to the pain and humiliation. The shorter of Mary's bullies slapped her face. Her mouth bled again, but she deprived the man of seeing her anguish. Junior, the second-largest vigilante, largest save for Eamon, kicked Woodson again. "We gonna give you the same kind of chance than you give James," he said before slapping Leonard's groping hands away from Mary's breasts. "Watch this, Blasingame," he said while reaching into Mary's now torn and partly unbuttoned blouse with both of his meat hook sized hands. Junior squeezed hard. Mary's face offered no response. Junior slapped her across the face and neck, harder than before.

The pain from the kicking almost blinded Woodson. For a few seconds he saw white, nothing else, and as his vision cleared, he thought *I got to save Mary, if I can. No hope for Calvin and me, but...*Eamon punched Woodson's stomach hard. It didn't hurt. Nothing hurt and his mind cleared. Woodson stood as straight as he could and said, "No way would James Callahan allow the death of a neighbor's wife to hang around his neck for all eternity. You know that. I know that. God knows that. James Callahan knows that, too.

Eamon's voice sounded above the din. "Woodson's right. James Callahan don't want no dead woman tied to his good name. Turn her loose."

Junior shoved Mary away. "Next time I'll pull your tits clean off, Squaw! That or cut 'em off!" Mary covered her breasts as best she could with her torn blouse. She then spat in Junior's face. Junior's right hand became a fist, and he took a single step toward Mary before Eamon grabbed his shoulder.

"Junior, get away from her! She didn't kill nobody!"

"She spit on me!" shouted Junior, who did as Eamon said. He then returned to the rail and kicked Woodson twice, once in the stomach and once across the bridge of the nose. Blood poured from Woodson's broken nose as Junior said, "I got a good mind to nut you before you die, Blasingame!"

Woodson and Calvin tried to stand. Neither could. Woodson cursed as Calvin pointed to the man who abused both his mother and father. With blood gurgling in his throat, Calvin growled, "You ain't worthy of touching either one of them's feet!"

Eamon stepped between the Blasingames and Mary's tormenter. "Junior, get your ass back from there or I'll drag you in the dirt!", rumbled from Eamon's throat. Junior did as he was told. Eamon dropped to one knee. Woodson thought Eamon's throat and groin had to ache as he heard a raspy voice. "I'm tryin' to save her life with no help from your big mouth, you stupid shit."

"Show me," whispered Calvin.

Eamon stood and shouted to the other vigilantes, "Make a path between me and the horses." The mob separated and a clear path opened from the hitching rail to the animals. He cut the lashes from Mary's wrists, grunting once in the process. "Need to put an edge on this damn knife, he muttered before turning toward the mob. "I'm freein' Mrs. Mary to go to them horses," Eamon called with a still raspy voice. "She'll pick one, any horse she wants, and ride it away from here. Whoever owned it, it's hers now and we all are gonna let her and the rest of her family be. Anybody that don't like that can take it up with me, personal!" Nobody raised a complaint.

Mary didn't move. Eamon pointed to the horses across the road. "Run, to the horses, woman!"

"My place is here, with my husband and my son," Mary crossed her arms and stood still, defiant.

Eamon laid his hands on either side of his head and said, "Send her, Woodson. She won't go if you don't push her, and she'll die if she don't."

Woodson sat up and made a come to me motion with his left hand. When Mary knelt, he touched her cheek. "If you love me, get on one of those horses and go home. You got responsibilities there, responsibilities for you and me both. I ain't askin' you to leave for you. I'm askin' that you do it for me, for what's in my heart. That's you and our small children." She stood rigid, immobile. He pressured her. "Pick out a horse that Nancy'll think is pretty and ride it out of this Hell hole, Mary! Go like the Devil was after you!"

Thomas Johnson, his face ashen and hands trembling, dropped to both knees beside Mary. He gripped her dress hem with both hands and said, "Mrs. Blasingame, my roan mare is in the middle over there. Hilda, you've seen her before; she's a good horse and I give her to you. Ma'am, please, please take her and when you get home..." He took a deep breath. "Sarah...I..." He wept, left his words hanging.

Mary touched Thomas's neck and shoulder. She asked, "Tell Sarah what, Thomas?"

Thomas shivered and stood before he spoke. "I don't... I don't... I didn't..." He looked at Mary, then at Woodson. "I'll walk you to Hilda, help you get in the saddle." He started toward the horse.

Mary watched Thomas for a few seconds before turning her attention to her husband. She knelt beside him. "I'll do as you ask, Woodson," she said. Her voice was soft, accepting. "I'm leaving now." She stood and turned toward the mob. Mary stared at Eamon, then at Junior, then at each vigilante one at a time before she spoke again. This time she spoke louder, in a more forceful tone. "I'm not worried about the Devil chasing me, he's busy here tonight!" She then mouthed to her husband and son, "I love you." With unyielding and defiant steps, Mary walked, she did not run, and held her head high as she passed through the parallel lines of vigilantes. Thomas met her beside Hilda. She waved away his offer to help as she mounted the mare. Thomas folded his arms across his chest as Mary rode toward home at a steady pace, not as though the Devil was in pursuit.

Thomas returned to the other vigilantes near the porch. He neither made eye contact nor spoke with any of them.

"Thank God," said Woodson as Mary disappeared into a grove of Live Oaks.

Calvin lunged at Junior, who stepped between Calvin and Eamon. "You bastard!" Calvin shouted as three vigilantes pulled him back. Junior smiled while drawing his revolver. He killed Calvin with a shot through the forehead.

Woodson crawled, struggled to reach his son's body to no avail. Junior's second shot splintered Woodson Blasingame's sternum and drove him back to the ground. Woodson willed himself to one knee to no avail. He collapsed, died beside his son. Junior holstered his gun and in a curious act that could be nothing but justification for or absolution from what he had seen, Eamon bowed his head in silent prayer.

After the group said, "Amen" in unison, Junior's Amen was the loudest, Eamon said, "Thomas Johnson, most of us lost money at the hands of the Blasingames, but you lost both money and kin at the Blasingame place. Do you want to say anything?"

"Yes, there's something I want to say; something I need to do, too" answered Thomas. He stepped through the crowd, drew his father's revolver from his holster as he stood over Woodson and Calvin, and fired three shots into each dead Blasingame. Thomas stared at his smoking revolver for a long minute before holstering it and walking toward the line of vigilantes. They separated to accommodate him.

Seconds later, a barrage. perhaps a hundred shots, tore through the Blasingame dead. The magnitude of the assault overwhelmed Woodson and Calvin's bodies and released their pent-up blood, urine, and feces. The blood and waste pooled around father and son and stained the ground.

A tearful Thomas Johnson returned from the road and pushed his way onto the porch. He waved his arms while screaming at his fellow vigilantes, "I am a crazy bastard who just shot two dead men. All of you are crazy bastards, too! You shot the dead men, too! Why the Hell did we do it?" He drew his now empty revolver and inhaled its acrid residue before he continued, "We, that means me and all of you, killed two men tonight, men who defended their own! Every man here would have done the same!"

Eamon's voice was soft. "They killed your Daddy, son."

"Because James Callahan talked him into going out there to kill them! Callahan was a man with a bad temper and enough money to bend people to his way of thinking! Money made everybody forget about everything James said and some things he did. Let me tell you what separated the Blasingames from James Callahan! He had all the bad temper, except for Calvin sometimes, and damned near all the money! Us defending everything he did, including killing Lipan squaws and old men, is proof that money don't just talk in Blanco County, it screams!"

Not a vigilante spoke.

Thomas continued, "I'll have shame and a hole in my heart because of what you and me, and James Callahan's temper and money, did tonight! Not only did we kill men who defended their family and home, we put a wedge between me and the woman I love. That damned wedge will never go away, and she will hate me forever! That's the woman I wanted to marry who'll do that! Her contempt already shames me, makes me hate myself as much as I hate every one of you bastards!"

Eamon looked away. Junior looked like he wanted to say something but didn't.

Only distant night birds and a solitary owl somewhere in the trees across the road spoke as Thomas buried his face in his hands and leaned against the door. The boy holstered his gun. The vigilantes parted again when Eamon waved his right arm, a signal to open a path between the porch and the road. Thomas stepped from the porch to the hard dusty ground. He stared at the dead Blasingames for a few seconds and stepped into the road without speaking or looking back. He walked toward town, toward the family home behind the Mercantile Store. There his mother's tears and his father's last bottle of Rye whisky would comfort him.

TWENTY-TWO

**Going home, behind the Mercantile, Blanco County,
Texas
Monday, April 14, 1856, 9:15 PM**

A dozen quiet vigilantes mounted their horses almost as one and rode toward the Boggus Saloon. In the distance, well to his rear, Thomas heard the clop of horses' hooves and the uneven squeal and squeak of a buckboard. The sounds grew louder, neared him from behind, as he walked down the center of the road without looking back.

Where a sign proclaimed the town limit, about a third of the way from the JP Office to Boggus' well-lit bar, Thomas sensed as much as he heard the riders' horses slowing gait and changing position. They no longer sounded clustered behind him; now the clopping sounds locations were different. Now they came from separate rows behind and on either side of him, perhaps ten yards to his east and west. Only the buckboard's intermittent discordant squeal seemed close behind him now. Thomas refused to turn and look. He kept his eyes focused on the bright lights beaming through the Boggus' front windows. Now almost marching, he looked neither left nor right as the lead riders of each line slowed to match his pace and walk their horses on both his East and West sides. A heavy silence flooded the boy. It seemed to capture the men flanking him and the trailing buckboard. Thomas knew Eamon Cox was in the wagon behind him. Only Eamon rode a buckboard to the JP office that night.

No vigilante spoke. It was as though the silence wouldn't allow it. The horses and their riders all seemed under a spell, caught in the moment, save for the solitary and relentless squeak of buckboard's complaining axles. The sound's pitch changed when Eamon tapped his reins across his team's backs. With a gentle pull on his left rein, he brought his wagon up to Thomas' side, perhaps five feet to the young man's left.

Thomas ignored Eamon. He continued to stare straight ahead, into the Saloon's bright lights.

Eamon voice sounded more like a plea than an offer when he broke the silence. "It's more'n a mile from here to the Mercantile, Thomas. How about letting me give you a ride home?"

Thomas didn't respond. His eyes remained locked on the Saloon. The lights seemed a little brighter and he could hear some sound in the distance now, saloon sounds.

Eamon kept his team's pace steady, matching Thomas stride for stride. After another quiet moment, Eamon said in a soft voice, "You didn't kill nobody, boy. If you're eating yourself up about that, you didn't do nothing, even though the Blasingames killed your daddy."

Thomas continued to stare straight ahead as he spoke for the first time. "Your face will be the first one I see in Hell."

Another silence. "Climb in the wagon. It ain't the best ride in the county, but it can get you where you're wantin' to go." Eamon sighed, "Dammit, Thomas, neither one of us knows whether either or both of us is going to Hell! You sure as shit ain't on Ol' Billy's list yet! Like I done told you, you didn't kill nobody tonight!" Eamon's voice took on a harsh tone. "Stop a minute and look at me, boy!"

The hard edge in Eamon's tone made Thomas stop. No emotion showed in his face as he stared at Eamon's.

Eamon sighed. He extended his right arm and pulled it across his body, a 'come on' motion. His words were soft, almost pleading, "Get up here! I'll take you home. I'll tell your momma you didn't do nothing, too. You want me to do that?"

"No." Thomas started walking before he answered. "I want to walk and be alone with my thoughts, Eamon. I don't need you or anybody else speaking to my momma on my behalf, either."

"He ain't interested," Claimed a voice from the vigilante row beside Eamon's buckboard. "Leave him be, Eamon. I want a drink," added another voice near the first.

Eamon nodded. He flicked the reins across his team's back once. As the horses accelerated to a trot, he called over his shoulder, "That whiskey ain't goin' to drink itself, boys! Let's go get it!"

No vigilante said another word to Thomas. Eamon looked back once. The boy's image seemed to fade into the dust cloud their horses raised.

TWENTY-THREEE

Blasingame home, Blanco County, Texas
Monday, April 14, 1856, 9:30 PM

Mary pulled Hilda to a halt at the hitching rail between her and the front porch. She blotted her eyes. "Sarah, Luther…" she called.

Mary heard elation in Sarah's voice as her daughter stepped through the doorway. "Momma!"

Luther, who stopped after taking a single step onto the porch, asked, "Momma, where are Daddy and Calvin? Why aren't they with you?"

Mary heard the concern in both their voices. She shook her head. "They're not coming." She gripped the saddle horn and dismounted. After Mary wrapped her reins around the rail once, she took a deep breath. "Columbus, Nancy…?" she asked.

"Asleep," answered Sarah. "I put them both to bed an hour ago." She stepped down from the porch and touched the horse's nose. "Hilda. Why did you ride Thomas' horse, Momma?"

"He gave her to me. I needed her to ride from the JP office."

Sarah stepped nearer to her mother. Mary winced as her daughter touched her face and neck. "Momma?" Sarah questioned. She turned to her brother. "Luther, come look at this."

Luther turned his mother's body so that the light through the front window gave him a clear view of her face and neck. "How'd this... What..."The sound of fearful understanding replaced questioning and concern in Luther's voice. "Daddy and Calvin...?" His voice trailed off.

"Gone; dead at the hands of a mob."

"The same people who did this to you?"

Mary nodded.

Luther talked fast. Mary recognized the rage in his questions. "What mob? Who was in it? Where was George Lange? Couldn't he stop them? Did he even try? Give me some names, all of them!"

Mary recognized that Luther was about to go for revenge then and there. She forced herself to speak in authoritative measured words, those of a matriarch with a damaged and endangered family. "Luther, you will not go off and get yourself killed tonight! You will sit, think, and talk with your sister and me while I share everything with both of you. After that, we will plan what we're going to do as a family and how we're going to do it."

Luther's shoulders seemed to relax. "Tell me something, anything, right now, Momma...I need something!"

"We'll go into the details in a few minutes, but I can tell you it was a crowd. It all kind of runs together on me as I think about it. I remember Eamon Cox, Junior Abbot, and Leonard Jacks. Other names will come to me. Eamon did most of the talking."

"Lange?" pressed Luther. "Was he there?"

"George was nowhere to be found. He disappeared into thin air before they come to pull us out into the street. He was gone and only God knows where before anything happened."

Luther asked, "Him being the JP and not being there don't

sound right. Any indication that he was he in on it?"

Mary sensed that Luther was becoming agitated again. She kissed his cheek before answering. "Don't know either way. He might have been in league with them. That or scared of them. Could be either, neither, or both." A sob lurched from her son's throat. Mary took him in her arms, held him close. Neither spoke for over a minute. When Luther seemed controlled, Mary rested a hand on each of Luther's shoulders, squeezed them with a gentle touch, and kissed both of his cheeks. A look into Luther's eyes told her that he was with her again. He wouldn't run off and do anything stupid tonight. "Take Hilda to the barn and tend to her. Sarah and I will put some coffee on. The three of us have a lot of talking to do tonight."

Luther pulled the looped rein from the hitching rail. He rubbed Hilda's neck and whispered, "Let's go to the barn, Hilda. We're having a bad day, the worst ever around here, but that don't mean I won't see to you tonight. Let's go on to the barn, girl. I'll make you comfortable."

Mary embraced Sarah as Luther and Hilda disappeared around the house. Sarah wept in her mother's arms.

TWENTY-FOUR

**Johnson family home, behind the Mercantile, Blanco County, Texas
Monday, April 14, 1856, 9:45 PM**

Amy Johnson lit an oil lamp before sitting on the porch. A touch of dry dust rose from the ground as she planted her feet and rested her elbows on her knees. She sighed, held her head with both hands, and struggled to control her racing mind. *It's quiet, too quiet since the gunfire.* She remembered three distinct bursts: the first was two shots. The second was six, and the third many, many more., too many to count. Fear flooded her eyes with tears. *Dear God, why did Thomas go with those crazed fools to the JP office? Ain't nothin' going to bring his daddy back!*

A sound. Amy heard a sound, footsteps, somebody in the alley between the Mercantile Store and the Ladies' Millinery. She raised her head, squinted her eyes as she looked for light or motion near the sound. There was neither, but a lack of sound or temporary motion didn't mean no one was there. Someone moved in the center of the alleyway. Amy's oil lamp showed her the outline of a male nearing her. "Thomas?" she called.

"It's me, Momma," He walked into the light. His stride was

slow. It seemed pained, confused, to his mother.

Relieved and frightened, Amy said. "I heard gunshots, a lot of them. Did they, did you…?

Thomas leaned down and kissed his mother's cheek before sitting beside her. Neither spoke. Amy saw a distant, detached look in her son's eyes during the quiet long minute that followed. She thought, *Is he trying to figure out what to say, how to tell me something? Oh, dear God!*

"Momma, I'm going to tell you everything, but first I want to pour myself some of daddy's Rye Whiskey. Should I pour one for you, too?"

"Yes," she answered. "The bottle is behind the green beans I put up last summer."

"I know where it is…" Thomas voice trailed off as he stood and entered the house. He soon returned with a corked bottle and two glasses, each a third full of Rye Whiskey. He handed one to his mother and held the other in a firm grip as he sat beside her.

Another silence followed. Amy knew pain when she saw it, and she reached out and took his hand. She wanted to comfort him if she could.

Thomas sounded calm as he said, "My life is as good as over, Momma. I was as bad as any of them, crazy and bad. How bad was that? I was bad enough to know I'll go to Hell when I die."

Amy rubbed her son's hand. "Thomas…"

"No, Momma!" He swallowed hard and shook his head with quick side to side jerks. "I got no doubt about that! None! And when I get there, on the evil side of Judgement, the first faces I'll see are Daddy's and James Callahan's. Then I'll see every vigilante who was at the JP Office tonight. We'll all burn together!"

Amy's chest tightened. She hurt even more for her son. "What happened and what did you do at the JP office, Thomas? Did you kill any Blasingames?"

"No, Momma. Junior killed them. What I did was something only a man with a sick mind would do. I shot both Woodson and Calvin after they were dead. I shot them three times apiece! How crazy is that?"

Amy thought of the sets of shots she heard, first two and then six and then the barrage. "I heard a lot more shots than that, a lot more!"

"Every man there, the whole group of them, shot Woodson and Calvin after that; they fired maybe a hundred shots, maybe more. They, we, were like wild animals!"

"What about Mary Blasingame? I know she was there, too. What happened to her?"

Thomas' eyes looked deep, pained. "Eamon Cox let her go. I gave her Hilda so she could ride home. That's why I'm walking tonight."

Amy struggled to understand. "Were any of the other Blasingame children there? Did any of them see what happened tonight? Luther? Sarah? Please God, none of the little ones..."

"No, Ma'am," answered Thomas. "No small children, no Luther, and no Sarah." He took a deep breath before adding, "Sarah! Ain't no secret I been sweet on Sarah Blasingame for some time now." He paused. It appeared to Amy that Thomas stared into his past, present, and future. "I hoped..." His voice broke and he tried to collect himself before he continued, "I hoped someday that me and Sarah would... well, marry and have a family of our own."

Amy groped for something to say, words to comfort her son in a horrible time and place. "She's a sweet child..."

"Me and her," said Thomas in a raspy voice, He shook his head side to side. It was an absolute gesture. "That ain't going to happen now!" Thomas swallowed his Rye Whisky in a single gulp. He shivered once.

Amy blamed the whisky. *Poison* she thought, but she said nothing. She then forgave the Rye. *Sometimes a little poison is good for the soul.*

Thomas spoke again. His voice sounded mellow, calm, as he said, "Miss Sarah will hate me for the rest of my life, or hers, whichever of us dies first. That's a fact."

Thomas' mother handed her untouched whiskey glass to her son. "We lost your father. Mallheel was more sinner than saint, but he had some good in him. I loved him, accepted him, too. As for you, you lost a future with a wonderful young woman! Everybody around, all of Blanco County, lost good men and dependable neighbors in Woodson and Calvin Blasingame. Misery born of the devil! Nothing but misery came from any of it, nothing, and I have more to face as a middle-aged woman with a store I don't know how to run."

"I can run it, Momma. I watched Daddy enough, took part enough, to run it right." Tears again welled in Thomas' eyes. "I promise you this Momma: I'm gonna run the store and take care of you from now on. That's a promise!"

Amy gripped her son's knee, worried about the near future and that far away, and offered a half smile as she did so. "We will have each other, Thomas."

TWENTY-FIVE

Boggus Saloon, Blanco County, Texas
Monday, April 14, 1856, 9:30 PM

At the Boggus, they vigilante riders dismounted and tied their horses to the hitching rails. They climbed both steps between the ground and the saloon's porch and pushed the swinging doors. They entered two abreast. Once on the sawdust strewn floor, some looked toward George Lange's favorite table. There he was in his favorite chair. It faced the bar and gave him an unobstructed view of the whiskey shelved in tiers along the glass wall behind it and ample opportunities to stare at his dream girl: the lovely woman he knew as Miss Cleopatra Goodbody.

George's left elbow slipped off his chair's armrest. He struggled and succeeded in sitting upright again. One watching vigilante said aloud, "If that ain't drunk, I've never seen it."

The man beside him said, "My guess is we'll see a lot of that from George between now and doomsday."

The vigilante who first spoke answered, "Doomsday's here. We saw it."

The other riders agreed.

TWENTY-SIX

Blanco County and German Cemeteries
Sunday, April 20, 1856, 2 PM

County officials declared Woodson and Calvin as 'undeserving deceased' and denied their family permission to bury them in the community cemetery.

A unified German community shared the cost of two plots in the Sauer family section of their cemetery and offered them to Mary, Luther, and Sarah.

The Blasingames accepted.

Saint Martin's Lutheran Church memorialized both father and son an hour before their burial.

TWENTY-SEVEN

German Cemetery, Blanco County, Texas
Saturday, November 1, 2025, 5:30 PM

Neither grandchild moved as Gree continued, "George Lange and seven others faced charges and Blanco County tried them one at a time." She looked wistful, almost smiled as she added, "There were no convictions. Only one case, the last one, ended with a hung jury and that was after several changes of venue."

An indignant Jojo exclaimed, "I cannot believe that nobody went to jail!"

"Your Grandpa's cousin Clyde was a lawyer. He used to say, 'if you want justice, go to church'." Gree sighed before continuing, "It'll be dark soon. Let's start for the motel."

As his grandmother unlocked the car, Logan asked, "What happened to Mary?"

"She and her children moved away the next year. Nobody knows where or what happened to her, but that doesn't end her story."

"What else happened?" asked Logan.

"Years later, a German girl told her mother she heard a woman's voice calling her dead family in the cemetery. The mother heard it too; she said it was weak or far in the distance. She said she recognized Mary Blasingame's voice as soon as she heard it."

Jojo folded her arms. "The thought of calling dead people gives me goose bumps! Does she still do it?"

"Yes, but it's rare. The story is she only calls on clear nights with west wind strong enough to carry a voice but having those conditions doesn't mean she'll use them and call. If she calls, well, it'll be when she wants somebody, usually Woodson is my guess."

A suspicious Logan asked, "The voice. Has anybody else said it's her?"

"I understand a number of people over the years, but nobody I know. All I know is what's called common knowledge."

Now curious, scared, and playful, Logan said, "It's getting dark, and the sky is clear. Can we hang around another few minutes?"

"Not a chance," answered Jojo while pushing him into the back seat.

Appendix

THE *AUSTIN STANDARD* NEWSPAPER PUBLISHED
THIS EDITORIAL AFTER THE TRIALS

"We are satisfied that no one who participated in causing the death of the Blasingames, but will, in cooler moments, deeply regret the course he has taken. We cannot tell what were the just desserts of the prisoners, but this we know, and this every freeman will assert --that so long as there was an opportunity to appeal to the judicial tribunal, he should have beent tried by a jury of his counttrymen, and the proper verdict rendered by them.

This sad even will go abroad to misrepresent the character of our people...We may well say that this event would have never transpired, could it have been forseen by the leading citizens of Hays, in time to have interferred. We hope never again to be called on to record another scene of the kind in this county."